A CORSICAN TALE

JANE CORBETT

Beggar Books

First published in 2022 by Beggar Books

A CIP catalogue record for this book is available from the British Library

ISBN: 978-1-910852-79-8
eISBN: 978-1-910852-78-1

Cover image and design by Jamie Keenan
Typeset by yenooi.com

A CORSICAN TALE

Three weeks after burying her mother, Jessie boarded the night ferry from Marseille to L'Île-Rousse on the west coast of Corsica. She'd slept most of the way on the TGV from Paris, which was probably a good thing since she hadn't reserved a cabin. Still, as it was only early June the ferry wasn't full and there'd be plenty of benches to stretch out on.

Her mother's death from colon cancer had been fairly rapid, which was a mercy. She'd moved into her house to look after her during the last desperate weeks, a time to say some of the things she'd left unsaid for years and for which therefore she was grateful. It wasn't exactly a beautiful ending but as she clung to the bird bones of that fragile hand, she knew that grief would be stronger than regret.

The following week she kept herself busy, clearing up the house as best she could, ready to put it on the market when she returned from the break she planned once this was all over. She felt exhausted and numb, reluctant to see anyone and unable to focus on what to do next or whether she'd even have a job to go to. The head of the legal chambers where she worked as a family lawyer, had called the day before the funeral with her commiserations, and suggested that in the light of further cuts to legal aid she should continue her leave till September. By then, she hoped, things would have picked up.

She left checking her old attic bedroom till last. To her knowledge it hadn't been slept in in years, but she felt reluctant to disturb what youthful relics might remain.

It was empty, except for a bed, a small desk, a chair, and a cupboard. She opened the cupboard and saw it contained a few of her old belongings - the guitar she'd picked up for a few months then abandoned when the girl band they were planning failed to materialise, and a few old clothes that for some reason her mother hadn't given to charity. On the shelf there was a suitcase. When she took it down, it felt light and at first she thought it was empty. But when she opened it her stomach clenched in recognition. Inside was an old diary and a pipe carved out of willow with holes for stops, wrapped in an old sock.

She recognised the diary at once. She'd written it when she was sixteen during three weeks spent in Corsica, and hidden it away on her return. Finding it now chimed uncannily with a dream she'd had only the other night. An old woman was calling to her in a language she didn't understand. At first she thought she was angry, then her voice softened and a moment later the woman turned and walked away. A feeling of intense desolation woke her and she found tears running down her cheeks. At the time she'd associated the old woman with her mother. But her mother was slight and still youthful, despite her sickness, whereas the woman in the dream was strong and forceful, and her mind went back to Corsica. For over an hour she sat on the bed, the open diary on her lap and the pipe resting between her hands, as one memory surfaced after another.

When eventually she got up and left the room, she knew where she wanted to go. Instead of the Greek island she'd been contemplating, she would revisit Corsica. A friend had returned from there last summer, having stayed with people who owned a large house in a mountain village above Calvi. She'd raved about the island's wild mountains and empty beaches, especially beautiful in spring and early summer.

It was more than twenty years since her previous visit, and at the time she'd thought never to return. But now, after all these years, she was a different person, and perhaps it was time to revisit the place that had so marked her adolescence. She had almost two months at her disposal and could rent a room from the people her friend had mentioned. She looked down at the diary and the pipe she held in her hand, relics from a past she'd done her best to push to the edges of her consciousness, still waiting to be laid to rest. Perhaps she could bury them in the soil from whence they'd sprung.

On the ferry she found a bench, which she commandeered with her suitcase and went in search of something to eat. The only place serving food was a small canteen on the lower deck, offering croque monsieur - a white poached egg on a piece of flaccid white bread. As there was no other option, she bought one and went back to her seat.

She pulled the teenage diary she had saved for the journey out of her bag, and opened it at random. It took a moment before she felt able to focus her eyes on the page. She took a bite of her croque monsieur and began to read.

Today is my 3rd day of captivity. Yesterday I managed secretly to break off a tiny piece of soap from the big lump in the kitchen without the woman noticing. A bit later I persuaded her to let me take some hot water from the copper on the range to wash my hair and clothes, which were filthy. I had to wash my clothes just before I went to bed, tipping the water away out of the window when I'd finished and hanging the clothes out to dry on the back of the chair and the bedrail because I've nothing else to wear. In the morning they were still damp when I came to put them on. I stood near the range whilst I ate my breakfast, shivering and steaming, hoping they'd dry quickly before I caught my death of cold. It gets quite chilly at night and in the early mornings up here in the mountains...

But the lavatory is the worst thing of all. It's in an outhouse, a wooden seat suspended over a stinking pit with the flies constantly buzzing round it. The first time I went there I thought I was going to be sick, and even now I never go until I'm forced to. I'm getting more used to it though — they say human beings can get used to anything! I take a deep breath just before I go in, then breath very lightly through my mouth. While I'm sitting there I cover my head with my arms to keep off the flies.

That way it isn't nearly so bad. Of course there isn't any paper and I don't want to use up too many pages of my notebook.

After a couple of bites, Jessie abandoned the croque monsieur, got up and threw it in the nearest waste bin. She sat down again, turned over a couple of pages and resumed her reading.

Thursday (I think it is, though it's hard to keep track of the days here). Every morning when I get up, the men have already left the house, which is a relief. The woman gives me breakfast of goat's milk, which I've got used to now, and little fried cakes made out of chestnut flour: they are delicious. Then I spend most of the day helping the woman out with the chores, fetching water, scrubbing pots, cleaning and preparing vegetables for the evening meal, and other chores. I hate them but it's better than being idle, I suppose. It leaves me less time to think. The woman herself works like a donkey all day, milking and tending her goats, making their milk into cheese, peeling and pounding chestnuts into flour, cooking bread, soups and stews.

The job I hate most is peeling chestnuts. The sharp husks cover your fingers with a mass of little painful cuts and the fleshy part never wants to come away from the shell. It reminds me of Wales, of making the stuffing for the Christmas turkey. The first time I had to do it, I could hardly stop myself from sobbing out loud, I felt so terribly homesick. But I stopped myself because I don't want the woman to know how bad I feel and how frightened I am. If she thinks I'm bearing up all right, she may be inclined to treat me with more respect and leave me alone. After about half an hour, she saw that I hadn't even finished half the bowl of chestnuts and was very annoyed. She took the bowl from me, saying something in a cross voice which as usual I couldn't understand, and handed me a bowl of apricots to stone instead. I ate quite a few of them whilst she was outside working in her vegetable patch. Serve the mean old bag right! I could see her through the window with an old straw hat on her head, digging away in the stoney earth. She'll be lucky if she gets much to grow in that soil!

Friday. Today, my fifth, I have been allowed out for the first time. The woman let me help her in the vegetable garden this morning. Digging in that soil is backbreaking work but it's lovely to be out in the fresh air and see the sky. I looked round at the surrounding mountains and thought again that there's nowhere to run to, only empty space. Sometimes I can't believe any of this is really happening...

It's no good just feeling sorry for myself. I've got to try and survive somehow until I'm rescued. The best way is to distract myself from my troubles. So I'll start by describing the house. ...

She closed her eyes, back once more in the kitchen of that remote farmhouse with its smoked hams and bunches of herbs hanging from the ceiling, its cooking range, large oak table, and kegs of wine and oil stashed away in one corner. The oil was a beautiful greenish gold and had a tarry smell she'd come to love when she dipped Mama's homemade bread into it. She'd begun to call the big woman Mama because that's what her sons called her and she heard no other name.

The ones she'd most feared were the two older brothers, partisans in one of the various nationalist movements that controlled the island. She couldn't recall their faces because she'd been too afraid to look at them and stuck close to Mama whenever they were around, doing her best to be invisible. But when she closed her eyes she could still see Paolo's face quite clearly, his handsome looks and gentle smile that had been her undoing.

She'd agreed to go for a stroll with him along the beach, when she was seized upon by his brothers and taken into captivity. It didn't matter they'd mistaken her for the daughter of her friend's successful father, the British MP with whose family she was on holiday. They assumed that as a well-known, wealthy public figure, he'd pay the ransom they demanded. And no doubt, being an honourable man, he'd have done so.

... On the other hand the family seem to think nothing of clothes. They only appear to own two sets of clothes each, one for ordinary wear, one for best. Once the two older brothers got dressed up to go out in the evening. They looked ridiculous, almost unrecognisable in dark, old-fashioned suits with their hair brushed flat, and they walked in a funny stiff way. It certainly didn't improve their appearance. Paulo only goes mooching out with his dog. He's quite a lot younger than the others and seems rather turned in on himself. But I'd rather not think about him.

In the evening after supper it's very quiet with no radio or TV. The mother mends or patches the men's clothes and sometimes she knits, on big needles with unbleached wool. The smell of the wool reminds me of the tufts I used to collect from the fences and hedgerows in Wales, and I get terrible bouts of home-sickness. Sometimes I feel so desperate I think I may go mad. Mum must be frantic with worry. And what about the Taylors? Have they got the ransom message yet? Are they managing to raise the money?

She skipped the next couple of pages and came to entries she had written after she returned home, so she would not forget.

One morning I was in the kitchen scouring the milk pan, when Paolo appeared. Mama was in the outhouse making cheese. I could see he wanted to talk to me but I ignored him. I'm still too angry to be friendly. Eventually he said in his ridiculous English, 'I make something for you.' Despite myself, I wiped my hands on my apron and turned to look at him. He was holding out a pipe, about the size of a recorder with holes for stops, deco-rated all over with a carved pattern of leaves. I could see he'd taken great pains making it.

'It's for you to play,' he said. 'When your work is finished. A voice of your own.'

Of course, he would go and spoil his gift by saying 'When your work's finished...'.

But one thing is true. Bit by bit the pipe has become a kind of voice. At least a way of expressing some of those pent-up feel-ings I've no way of talking about, and anyway no one to talk to.

. . .

She stuffed the diary into her wheeled suitcase and zipped it up. There was no chance of sleep. The lounge felt stuffy with the breath of snoring sleepers and the occasional whimper of a wakeful child. She went out through the far doors to the rear deck, but that was full of animated people, drinking and talking loudly. She walked back the way she had come and along a corridor lined with small shops, closed now because it was late. Eventually she noticed a door with a light above it that said Cinema. It was unusual for a ferry and probably only showed cartoons for children and the odd newsreel. But still that was better than the lounge.

The small auditorium was empty, except for a pair of entwined lovers in the back row, who seemed to have fallen asleep. She made her way to the front and sat down, propping her case against the seat beside her. The film had just started, and she watched hypnotised as a couple of men struggled with the waves to land a small boat laden with a piano to the shore. A woman and child stood on the beach, observing them. Though you could only see them from behind, you felt the tension in their bodies as they watched, holding one another tightly by the hand, and all the while haunting, repetitive music from a piano mingled with the sounds of sea and wind.

At eight a.m. the ferry docked at L'Île-Rousse. The sun was just rising above the promontory that gave the town its name, flushing the red earth with hints of gold. Families waiting to greet loved ones thronged the quayside, and on the far side of the quay, cars were lining up to go aboard once the ferry had discharged its cargo.

Jessie followed the line of foot passengers and made her way down the gangway and straight to the nearest car hire office. She decided on a Clio, the cheapest car on offer, signed the papers, and joined the queue of cars heading up from the harbour to the high road that ran north/south along the coast. It was slow progress but when eventually she reached the roundabout at the top, she saw a sign to the right that said Calvi.

She'd slept for a while in the cinema after the film ended, and in the morning, unable to linger in a toilet trashed and sullied during the long night, merely splashed her face with water and did a brief tooth clean. She felt tired and jaded, and the sun was already getting hot. She wound down the windows for some air.

The road ran high above a narrow coastal plain, rising steeply on the other side towards the mountains. Below the road, wide sandy bays were interrupted here and there by clusters of low buildings and a campsite. It wasn't the kind of development that blighted so many Mediterranean coastlines, but neither was it the wild beauty she'd been led to expect. What she most needed was a decent coffee and some breakfast, and since there was no sign of a café along the road, she turned inland at the next opportunity.

A steep incline led to a village square. On one side was a flight of stone steps and a large Romanesque church, complete with a campanile. Behind that a maze of tiny streets scrambled up the hillside to foothills that fringed the mountains. The sea side of the square was bordered by plane trees and looked out towards the bay and the shore below. Tables were laid out under the trees, and across the road was a café. Jessie parked her car and approached the tables. Two of them were already taken, one by a group of men talking animatedly in Corsican, the other by a couple of backpackers, blonde girls who looked Dutch or Scandinavian. They were pretty but the men ignored them, and it took her some time to attract the attention of the waiter, who was conversing with the men at their table. Eventually he arrived to take her order, and when he turned away to the café, the Corsicans got up too and accompanied him back across the road, where they settled in at the bar.

When eventually the waiter returned with a large café crème and a baguette with cheese and ham, she began to feel more cheerful. She ordered another coffee and whilst waiting for it to be delivered, went over to the small shop at the corner of the square in search of a newspaper. She'd hoped for a French paper, perhaps Le Monde, but there was only the local Corse Matin. She bought a copy since at least it would be good for her French, and returned to her table.

As she drank her second coffee, she perused the paper. On the front page was a story from Bastia, a port on the east coast and capital of the north. It described how a well-known criminal, who was being transported by police van less than half a kilometre from the gaol to the court house, had escaped. He'd subsequently managed to evade recapture and the trial was therefore cancelled. She smiled to herself with a mixture of bitterness and amusement. The law, it seemed, was still in thrall to whatever powers ran the local region, whether political or criminal. Little had changed in the twenty-odd years since she was last here.

Revived by her breakfast, she rejoined the coast road and a few kilometres before Calvi turned inland. At the next roundabout she saw a signpost saying Montegrosso, the group of villages towards which she was headed. The name was almost unreadable because the sign was riddled with bullet holes.

After a couple of hundred metres, eucalyptus trees that had bordered the road gave way to open maquis, and through the window came the scent of the curry plant. Tall clumps of wild flowers were interspersed with ancient olive trees, and in the distance a line of stunted oaks marked the course of a small river that made its way down from the mountains up ahead. Then, as the road bent to accommodate a huge tree covered in yellow blossoms that half buried an old house, the car filled with the heady perfume of mimosa.

She crossed a bridge over a small river and the road began to wind upwards ever more steeply. Ahead she could see the village perched above her like a fortress at the end of the ridge. She changed into second gear and, at the final bend, down into first, and pulled up in the square.

Like most Corsican villages it had been built some way from the coast to protect it from the ships that never ceased to pillage the island. On the side facing the sea a line of tamarind trees gave shade. In the centre was a large Romanesque church with its flight of steps and campanile, typical of the region. The road made a circuit around the church, then continued on towards the next village and the mountains. To the right of the square, a cluster of small streets scrambled their way to the furthest edge of the ridge and a magnificent view across the valley.

The house Jessie was headed for was at the end of a terrace of tall houses, facing towards the back of the church, with a partial view of the sea. Its heavy front door was cracked and faded by years of sun and wind and there was no bell, only a ringed handle and a brass knocker in the form of a young girl's ringed hand holding a ball. Jessie rapped loudly, hearing the sound echo through the house on the other side. When there was no reply, she took hold of the heavy handle and turned it. With an additional shove, the door opened inwards and she stepped into a hallway from which rose a curved stone staircase.

Hearing no sound, she called out, 'Anyone at home?'

A man appeared on the first landing and called down to her to come up. He was in his sixties, tall and slightly portly with a rosy complexion and a thistledown cloud of white hair. He wore a loose shirt, canvas trousers and espadrilles, and gave a broad smile of welcome as he held out his hand.

'Forgive me! We didn't hear you arrive. I'm Douglas, and ...'

Before he could complete his sentence, another voice called out from the landing above, 'And I'm Ruth! Welcome to Corsica, Jessie!'

'The lady wife,' Douglas said, tilting his head upwards. 'Leave your suitcase down here for the moment and let's go up and have a drink, or coffee if it's too early for you.'

She followed him upstairs, where Ruth was waiting to

greet her in the doorway to their living room. She kissed Jessie on both cheeks and ushered her inside.

It was an elegant room, panelled, with a fine stone fireplace and a kitchen off to one side. The furniture was comfortable rather than elegant, and the place had the well-worn feel of a family house. French windows opened onto a terrace that ran two thirds the length of the room and faced onto the back of the church.

'Your friend, Julie, called yesterday, just to tell us when to expect you and to give us the number of your portable (she used the French term for mobile) in case you got lost. It seems you had no trouble getting here.'

'The ferry was on time. It even had a cinema! Not something I've encountered before.'

'Good films, but terrible food! Did you have breakfast?'

'I stopped at a café.'

'Come to the terrace,' Douglas said. 'It's shady in the morning and we can introduce ourselves.'

'D'you prefer coffee or something stronger?' Ruth asked.

'Coffee, please.'

She disappeared into the kitchen and Jessie followed Douglas onto the terrace. He gestured her to a seat around a long oak table.

'This is a magnificent house,' she said. 'How long have you lived here?'

'In this house nearly forty years. In Corsica, almost fifty.'

'So what brought you here? You're from America, I believe.'

'Canada. It's a long story.'

'I'd love to hear it.'

Ruth brought coffee, with some delicious macaroon biscuits from a local bakery, and set them down on the table. He smiled his thanks to her, then continued his tale.

'In my youth I fancied myself as a sailor. I had a friend, who was a real sailor. You've heard of the Kon-Tiki, I guess?'

'That raft that crossed the Atlantic?'

He nodded.

'Our sea travels eventually brought us to this island and we both fell in love with it. After a few weeks, in need of funds, we hired a small passenger boat and began ferrying tourists from Calvi to the coastal nature reserve a bit further south. There was very little tourist trade back then and we had no license, but we teamed up with a local taxi driver. We landed people at a small jetty where they could climb up to the road, and he ferried them back to town. It kept us for a couple of years in food and drink.'

'And then?'

'Herman moved on and I met Ruth. '

'And you bought this house?'

He nodded, smiling.

'And the rest, they say, is history.'

Ruth had joined them and sat down.

'You should have seen it!' she said. 'Beautiful, but almost derelict! A hundred years ago ten families had lived here, plus a bakery. There's a photo from that time on the landing. And there was us, no money, a small child, and a massive project on our hands.'

'But you did it. The house is wonderful!'

Ruth nodded.

'Bit by bit. Douglas did it.'

'With a little help from our friends.'

He grinned and his face turned suddenly youthful.

The space allotted to Jessie was a small apartment entered from a half-landing on the other side of the staircase. It consisted of a kitchen, old-fashioned but well equipped, with a gas bottle for the cooker and heating water, and plenty of pans and cooking implements. From there a room with a dining table, four chairs and a divan in one corner led to a large terrace that looked out over the valley all the way to the mountains. From the right of the dining room a few steps led down to a small bathroom with shower and lavatory, and a bedroom that formed one side of the terrace and had a door opening onto it. It had once housed the oven for the bakery and was a charmingly eccentric space.

The next morning after an early breakfast she drove down to the sea, and parked the car under a cluster of umbrella pines. From there it was a short scramble down to the beach, a sandy bay bordered by rocks and a path that continued for miles along the coastline. There were barely half a dozen people on the sands. She laid out her towel and, shading her eyes from the light glistening on the water, sat gazing out to sea. Close to the shore the water was turquoise, turning deep cobalt blue further out. She took several deep breaths and felt the stress of the past few months slipping like a cloak from her shoulders.

When she could bear the heat of the sun no longer, she entered the sea and swam to the rocks and back. Afterwards she stretched out on the sand to dry like a seal in the sun, until eventually it got too hot and she decided to go home. On her way, she stopped off at the local supermarket and stocked up with enough food and drink to last her the rest of the week.

With the beauty of the place and the warm sun she woke to each morning and golden evenings that ended each long, lazy day, her energy was returning, and with it the physical stamina lost during the weeks of confinement with her dying mother. She felt she'd arrived in paradise. It was the light, especially, that captivated her, something she'd never forgotten from her time of captivity. Hour after lonely hour she'd spent, staring out of her bedroom window at the empty splendour of the land, watching it change from bright to dark as day turned to night. After the greyness of a northern winter, this was something she'd longed for. But the main reason for her return was to lay to rest the ghost buried in that abandoned, and now rediscovered, suitcase. It was a chance to erase once and for all the trauma of her adolescence, to rediscover that freedom of spirit that somehow had been left behind.

The first task was to find out in what remote region she'd been held prisoner, perhaps even to revisit it, though that might not be so straight forward. The mother of the family was almost certainly dead by now, and the last thing she wanted was to run into any of the brothers. She had very little to go on, except the name of the place on the east coast not far from Bastia, where she and her friends had stayed. That wasn't much help, since the farm she'd been taken to was somewhere lost in the wilds of the interior. It was possible Douglas and Ruth might be able to assist her, but that would involve telling them about her kidnap, which she was reluctant to do. She decided to postpone the whole thing for the time being. She was enjoying her holiday too much, the first in a long time. The rest could wait.

The following morning she drove to the river in the foothills of the mountains at Bonifatu. The river tumbled between steep, tree-lined banks, rushing over roots and around huge boulders to here and there form deep pools of clear, cold water. She took a picnic and a book and spent the day plunging into the icy water then lying out to dry on a flat, sun-warmed rock. Having eaten her food, she fell into a deep sleep, to be woken by the sound of children's voices as they descended the river on a home-made raft, and decided it was time to go home.

The day after she climbed up to an abandoned village, perched high above the sea on the crest of a hill below the mountains. It took forty-five minutes to reach it from the nearest road, and as she sweated and puffed her way up the rocky path that seemed never ending, stopping every ten or fifteen minutes to catch her breath, she thought of the people who'd lived there until the end of the Second World War. How fit they must have been to carry the goods they needed up these precipitous, stony paths, with only the help of a couple of donkeys.

At the top there was a square, overgrown with weeds and wildflowers, with a chapel that was locked but still, it seemed, in occasional use. There were a few other build-ings, a single storey market or community hall, and along a narrow street that led off the square small, squat houses, each with a barn at one side for the animals, half sunk into the earth. Their thick walls and stone slated roofs must have given shelter against the winds that battered without mercy, but in the end it had proved too much and the place was abandoned.

She sat down on a rock near the well, most likely dry now, on the far side of the square. For a moment she remembered the farmhouse where she'd spent those weeks of captivity. Until the discovery of her diary, she'd scarcely given the place a thought. But now images were filtering back. The family's life had also been one of endurance and hard labour, beyond anything she'd expe-rienced even in the days of their Welsh commune. But even those hardships must have been nothing compared with the life these people had led, and as the winter storms lashed and the well dried up, in the end they'd been driven to leave.

She returned to where she'd parked the car, and was alerted by the sound of horse's hooves coming along the road. She stood back to watch as a rider approached a gate that opened onto a tree-lined avenue, leading up to a large house. The rider leaned down to release the lock and when she saw he was having difficulty opening it, Jessie went to his aid. She managed to release the catch and pushed the gate open.

'Not an easy thing to manage from horseback,' she said in French.

'Thank you,' he replied. 'Without you I'd have had to dismount. And getting back up on this fella when he scents home isn't easy.'

She gazed admiringly at the horse, a beautiful bay of around seventeen hands.

'You like horses!' he said, following her gaze.

She nodded.

'I ride whenever I can. Though I've not had much chance lately.'

'You're from England?'

'You can tell from my accent?'

He smiled.

'The English are great riders.'

She hesitated, then said, 'I suppose you don't know of anywhere I could ride around here?'

'Unfortunately I only have this boy, and he doesn't take kindly to riders he doesn't know.' He paused. 'There is someone, though. A shepherd, Pierre Savone. He keeps horses over at Olmi-Capella. I've heard he sometimes takes people out. Cavaliers confirmés, of course.'

He pulled his mobile phone out of his pocket and scrolled quickly through various entries before pausing at one.

'There! Would you like to take his number?'

She took out her own mobile and copied it down.

'Good luck! And thank you again for your assistance.'

'Shall I lock the gate after you?'

'Please. If you would.'

He saluted her with his riding crop and disappeared up the avenue at a leisurely trot.

That evening she called Pierre Savone and arranged to be at his field near Olmi-Capella at ten the following morning. Douglas, who she ran into on the staircase, told her to leave at least an hour and a half for the journey, since though it wasn't that far, the way was circuitous and involved a steep climb over a mountain ridge.

She didn't have riding clothes so she dressed in her thickest jeans, a teeshirt, (under which Pierre had suggested she wore her bathing suit), low canvas boots, and a panama hat onto which she'd sewn tapes for tying under her chin.

At eight-thirty she set off, taking the road that led up from the village, following the line of the mountains. The road was empty except for the odd delivery van, making for one of the villages perched above it. Below each one was a cemetery of small, domed and white-washed houses for the dead. Here and there patches of blackened earth and burnt trees, relics of the fires that constantly ravaged the island, interspersed clusters of olive trees and scrubby pasture. Some fires were started by lightning but many, according to Douglas, were the work of man.

At length she came to a cluster of houses and a sign that said Speloncato. From there she turned right past an abandoned nunnery, and began the climb to the ridge. Sometimes she had to slow to a crawl for a cow wandering along the middle of the road, pausing now and then to graze from one of the verges. At length she reached the top and pulled into a parking area to take in the view. Far below lay Spelancato with its rooftops and campaniles and thick walls that protected it on the sea side of the town. From there the land descended in another dizzying drop all the way to the coast.

She returned to the car and set off again along the other side of the ridge. Here the landscape changed dramatically. Instead of scrubland there were lush fields shaded by ancient sweet chestnuts, where cows grazed and the occasional pig rooted contentedly. A little further down, the road ran through a village between houses so close together there was scarcely room for the car to pass. She noticed scrape marks on the walls on either side. A group of women were seated outside their houses, sewing or peeling vegetables. They looked up as she came by but made no greeting, and she was almost forced to a halt when a man and his dog ambled across the road without glancing in her direction.

The street descended towards a sharp bend, where the road turned to the left around a chapel that stood on a wide grassy ledge, with a fine view over the valley. As she continued, she saw ahead of her a large black horse standing still in the middle of the road. It was facing away from her but she expected it to move at the sound of the car's approach. When it didn't, she gave a gentle toot on her horn, and when that had no effect, she pulled up and got out of the car.

She could tell from his rather lumpy legs and scruffy coat that the creature was old, and wondered if he was deaf. As she came up to him, she reached out a hand and laid it on his neck. He turned his head with its greying muzzle towards her, and she saw from his milky gaze that he was blind. There was something indescribably touching about this great ruin of a beast standing in the middle of the road, unafraid yet uncertain where to go. Placing one hand on his mane and with the other giving him a light slap on the haunches, they made their way to safety at the side of the road.

She thought how the villagers must be used to him, like the cows that wandered the roads freely even at night. By some miracle most of these animals escaped being run over, which must, she thought, be because their presence was taken for granted even by the more reckless drivers, as though they had as much right to be there as any other inhabitant. It was an attitude she recalled from her time as a child in the Welsh commune, an instinctive connection between man and beast. And it was something she'd felt again in the rush of pride when, during her captivity, the mother had ordered her to milk the goat. At first the creature was restless and kicked out. But with time and patience she'd persuaded her to relax as she'd mastered the gentle rhythm of the pull, and her milk began to flow. As she drove on, she glanced into the rear-view mirror. The horse had put down his head and was quietly grazing.

At the next T-junction, she paused to consult her map. Ahead of her was a large, single storey modern building, surrounded by a walkway and on one side large double doors. It looked like some kind of public space, perhaps a theatre, though she couldn't think what a theatre would be doing in such a remote place. Less than a kilometre further on she spotted four horses in a field and an open-sided shelter, where a man was in the act of spreading out hay. This, she supposed, must be Pierre.

She parked the car at the roadside, and went over to introduce herself. He was of medium height, lean and dark and wore an English style cap. His face was lined and weatherworn, though he was probably barely fifty, and as he smiled and held out his hand in welcome, she knew she was in good hands.

The horse he gave her was a bay mare called Sylvane, a little over fifteen hands, strong but finely built, typical of the Corsican breed. Bags were attached to either side of her saddle, in which Pierre invited Jessie to put her belongings - water, sunscreen, and a small towel for bathing. He led the mare to a mounting block and as soon as she was in the saddle, she felt the deep thrill of connection with this febrile creature, so much stronger than her yet sensitive enough to feel her heartbeat.

They set off through fields of sweet chestnuts, until they came to open slopes that overlooked the valley and far below the river. The path ahead was narrow and stony, zigzagging its way down the hillside towards the river. Sometimes it descended gently, at others they were forced to circumvent an outcrop of rock or sudden cleft in the land. The horses scrambled for a foothold, their shoes sparking on the slippery rock, and Pierre called out to her that the mare knew what she was doing and to give her her head. It felt nerve wracking, but there was little alternative.

As the path resumed, he gestured up to a ledge on the hillside, so narrow it seemed to offer no foothold. A wild goat stood there, a large, sturdy creature with its dread-locks and massive horns.

'You don't often see mouflon these days,' Pierre said.

'Hunters?' she asked.

He nodded.

'It's forbidden, but …' He didn't finish the sentence.

When they reached the river, they waded through the water to avoid a small hump-backed stone bridge that Pierre said was Roman. On the other side the path became soft underfoot.

He turned back to her.

'Would you like a canter?'

She nodded, and the horses leapt into action, delighting in their sudden freedom.

At length they pulled up at a place where the river opened out to create a deep pool between massive boulders. Pierre suggested it was a good spot for a bathe and a picnic, so they entered the narrow strip of trees that separated the path from the water. They removed the horses' bridles and tethered them loosely to a couple of trees to graze, then climbed down towards the water. Pierre selected a flat rock and began to unpack parcels of food from his saddle bag.

'Would you like to bathe first?' he asked.

'Thanks! I shan't be long.'

She climbed down to the water's edge, took off her clothes, under which she had her bikini, and slid into the water. At first the cold took her breath away, but soon she was used to it, relishing its silky feel on her skin. She swam a couple of circuits of the pool, and felt a flutter against her leg as a fish darted past. A loud croaking came from a clump of reeds at the bank, and she caught sight of a huge frog squatting there, its throat swelling to a thin transparent membrane with each pulsating croak. It felt as though she'd entered some natural paradise and she wanted to go on swimming forever in this magical place.

Pierre was seated on the rock above, smoking a roll-up and gazing off in the direction of the horses. He gave no sign of impatience, never glancing in her direction, and she was enjoying herself so much she was in no hurry to get out of the water. A few minutes later, she heard the sound of male voices speaking in Corsican. She looked up and caught sight of a strange man, gazing down at her from a rock above. His gaze briefly met hers, then he turned away and there was the sound of low laughter.

Feeling a sudden chill, she waited for a moment then got out of the pool, wrapping her towel around her. She felt sure that with Pierre there she had nothing to fear. But still she was filled with unease. When she climbed back up to the bank, there was no sign of the other man. Pierre was alone, busy unwrapping the food and laying it out on the rock.

'I hope you've worked up an appetite.'

He indicated the feast spread out before her – bread, tomatoes, salami and his homemade sheep's cheese. Even a flagon of red wine from his neighbour's vineyard.

'It looks wonderful.' She paused. 'Who was that man I saw with you?'

He hesitated for a moment.

'Oh, him!' He shook his head. 'Just someone passing by. Please help yourself.'

The natural way he dismissed the incident reassured

her, and the laughter, she suspected, had come only from the other man. But still the feeling of unease did not quite leave her.

The picnic was delicious, and afterwards she went over to the trees where the horses were tethered, lay down on the soft earth and fell asleep. The sun was already past its zenith when Pierre woke her and she sat up startled.

'Goodness! How long have I been out?' she said apologetically.

'Almost an hour.'

'I'm so sorry. You should have wakened me.'

'The horses enjoyed the rest. And it seems you needed it,' he replied.

The ride home seemed easier, partly because it was uphill and partly because she'd become accustomed to her mare. Sometimes the path was wide enough for the two of them to ride side by side and they fell into conversation. She asked him about the large building she'd seen near the turning to Olmi-Capella, and he told her it was indeed a theatre. A friend he'd grown up with, a man called Simone Ranucci, had dreamed of having a theatre festival in this remote place, which meant having a building where people from all over the world, as well as locals, could come and participate. Ranucci had studied in Paris, working with a variety of well-known actors and writers. When he told them about his plan, they helped raise donations that enabled him to build his theatre. Now he ran a festival each year from the end of July to the beginning of September, and actors from all over the world came to perform. Jessie asked if she could buy tickets, and he told her to pick up a programme when she passed by on her way home or to look for the notice in Corse Matin. She was struck by how little the usual class distinctions appeared to matter on the island. Pierre, a local shepherd, was fully at home with a man like Ranucci, and if the books they'd discussed on their ride were anything to go by, he was about as well read as many a Paris intellectual.

When they reached his field, they untacked the horses, washed them down and fed them. She relished these tasks and felt she'd created a bond, however slight, with her mare. When it was time to leave, despite such a long day, she was reluctant.

'What do you do with the horses in winter?' she asked Pierre. 'I hear it gets cold up here, and you have no stables.'

'The horses come down to me in Belgodère,' he said, naming a town near the coast. 'That's where I have my permanent home.'

'It's a long way. Do you have a lorry?'

He shook his head. 'A long way by road but not down the mountain.'

'You mean you ride them?'

He shook his head. 'I lead them to the top of the ridge and let them go. They find their own way.'

'How long does that take them?' she asked, astonished.

'Rarely more than twenty-four hours. Often a lot less.'

Jessie was silent, marvelling at the intelligence and resourcefulness of these horses, and what trust in them Pierre must have.

'Can I come again?' she said. 'This day has been unforgettable. And I've fallen in love with Sylvane.'

He smiled.

'Any time. You have the number.'

That evening she knocked on the door of Douglas and Ruth's living room, eager to tell them about her day and to bring them some of the sheep's cheese Pierre had given her. They welcomed her inside with the usual offer of a drink, and introduced her to the young man standing beside them as their son, Simon (pronounced in the French way).

Simon had just arrived from Paris, the first of their three children who regularly spent the summer here.

'I hope I'm not taking up your space,' Jessie said.

He smiled. 'There's plenty of room. And I prefer it up in the attic.'

After a short conversation about Jessie's ride and the Ranucci theatre, Simon announced he'd arranged to meet up with friends in the village. As he bid her goodbye, he said he'd most likely run into her in the morning on the beach. Soon after he'd left she excused herself, scarcely able to keep her eyes open.

In the morning she got up early and drove the couple of miles to the sea. It was the perfect time, when the beach was still empty and the sun not yet too hot. She swam to where yellow buoys marked the safe edge of the bay and the start of more dangerous currents, and came back via the rocks. When she reached the towel she'd spread on the sand, she saw Simon had joined her.

'I was watching in case you went too far out,' he said. 'On calm days like this people often think there's no danger but there's a powerful undertow out there.'

'I'm not a strong enough swimmer to take risks.'

'Unlike Douglas. He used to swim from Calvi,' he gestured towards the town barely glimpsed in the hazy distance, 'all the way to the Mata Hari bay a couple of kilometres further down from here along the coast. He says he did it by floating on his back and letting the current bring him in for the last third.' He laughed. 'Still, it's not something I'd try.'

'He's quite something, that father of yours. A real adventurer!'

He nodded. 'Always keen to try something new!'

'Such people are rare. I guess it's his curiosity that keeps him so youthful.'

For a moment they sat in silence. At length he said, 'I hope you're enjoying yourself here.'

'Indeed I am. It's more beautiful even than I imagined.'

'Not much for entertainment though.'

'Which is another blessing!' She paused. 'You grew up here, so I guess to you it feels like home.'

'Even though I've lived in Paris since I was a student.'

'But you come back every summer?'

'And sometimes at Christmas. I guess like many Corsicans I'm something of a hybrid.'

'I understand that. I was brought up in Wales, in a commune. Part of me will always remain there, even though I could never go back.'

He smiled. 'Well, you'd better brace yourself for a taste of Corsican village life. The Fête des Olives is one of the highlights of our year, more important even than August 15th, Assumption Day. It takes place next weekend.'

'So what happens?'

'There are stalls with local artisans, crafts people and producers, including demonstrations from the olive pressers. And, of course, lots of music. People come from all over the Balagne.'

'Sounds great!'

He nodded. 'As long as you don't mind the noise. It used to be held outside the village in one of the neighbour's olive groves. Now they've moved it to the square and the stage is right outside our front door. You won't get much sleep.'

'I guess that's bearable for a night or so.'

'Wait till you hear it!'

By the beginning of the week before the fête was to open, lorries began arriving to deliver tables and chairs, a bar with lights strung through the trees was set up along one side of the square, and a stage was erected, as Simon had warned, outside the entrance to their house. The air of excitement in the village was palpable. The café on the far side of the church was stocking up with more boxes of food and drink than that small building could contain, so had to be carried down to a neighbour's cellar. Already its tables were filling up with strangers and it was doing brisk business.

On the following afternoon as she passed by, she saw Simon sitting there with a couple of friends. He called out to her to join them, and not wanting to appear rude, she did so. He introduced the two men and ordered her a beer. They were Corsican, and after a brief exchange of greetings, they soon ran out of polite remarks and reverted to the conversation they'd been having before her arrival. From time to time Simon made an attempt to include her, but since their French was so rapid and they talked about people she had no knowledge of, she was unable to follow. As soon as she'd finished her beer she stood up to leave.

One of the men was older than the other. He wore the characteristic black jeans and teeshirt and his head was shaved, a style favoured by many locals. As she bid them goodbye, he looked at her with an unsettling coldness. It was the same stare with which Ermano, the oldest brother in that family years ago, had regarded her, the same impersonal hostility that in some deep, irrational way seemed to reduce her to nothing. She turned and walked swiftly away.

On the Friday before the fête opened a concert of traditional voices was advertised, to be held in the church. Jessie knew very little about Corsican music but since this group was known as one of its finest, she decided to go.

Shortly before the concert was due to start, she went up to Douglas and Ruth and knocked on their door. Ruth opened it and welcomed her in. Douglas was seated at a low table opposite a man of around his own age, with short cropped grey hair and, unlike him, looked remarkably lean and fit. They were engaged in a game of chess.

'I didn't mean to disturb you,' Jessie said. 'I just wanted to know if you were coming to the concert tonight?'

Douglas looked up from their game.

'Jessie! How nice! This is Etienne Beauregard, my good friend and chess rival... Our prime aim is to finish our game. In any case, I'm afraid I've had my fill of Corsican music.'

Etienne stood up and offered Jessie his hand, before retaking his seat.

'If it's not chess that's obsessing them, it's their endless arguments,' Ruth said.

'I'd call them lively discussions,' Douglas replied. 'Etienne's a colonel at Camp Raffalli down there on the coast. Politically we may not always see eye to eye, but he's the most enlightened man I know.'

'And he's the most prejudiced,' Etienne replied. 'Though I admit he's also the most interesting and amusing.'

'So, a fine basis for friendship!' Jessie said.

They both smiled in response.

'Can we offer you a drink?' Ruth said. 'At least you can keep me company.'

'Thanks, but I'd better go and grab a seat, before the church fills up.'

It was the first time she'd been inside the church, which was usually kept locked. Though imposing on the outside, the interior was gloomy and bleak. The lofty stone walls were unadorned, except for a couple of undistinguished religious paintings and two plain glass windows set high up on either side of the nave. On the altar stood a statue of Mary in a blue robe with a lace shawl around her shoulders. In the alcove on one side of her was a much smaller figure of Christ, and on the other side John the Baptist. Before she came to Corsica Jessie had never seen Mary take precedence over her son, though that turned out to be common on the island.

The benches were already filling up. She made her way to the fifth row and took one of the two remaining seats at the end. The group, though internationally renowned, were originally from Calenzana, the small town across the valley, which made them local heroes, and from the buzz of anticipation they were the objects of both pride and a feeling of personal connection.

Eventually the hubbub died down and a tense hush fell over the audience, as six men dressed plainly in black jeans and teeshirts, emerged from the vestry. They formed a tight semicircle in front of the altar and each one cupped a hand over one ear, placing the other hand on the shoulder of his neighbour. Then they began to sing.

The sound was like nothing Jessie had ever heard. A deep hum that seemed to resonate through her whole body, a sound more felt than heard, growing ever louder and fuller, until at length a high, keening voice began to weave its way in and out of the other voices. They created incredible harmonies — something ancient with tones of Arabic music, plangent and unbearably haunting. The songs they sang were not romantic love songs, but rather spoke of love for the land that bore them, hymns of exile, death, and yearning, prayers for comfort from Mary, the Mother of all.

When it was finished and people began to get up from their seats to leave, she remained where she was until the last few had trickled out and the monitors were waiting to shut the doors. As one of them was packing up the CDs for sale into a suitcase, she hurriedly bought one, then paused on the church steps to gaze out over the bay. Through the velvety darkness the lights of Calvi blinked in the distance and far above, the great dome of the heavens was full of stars. She felt a profound sense of peace — calm but also invigorating, as though some new chapter were about to begin.

The following morning, she woke to the hum of voices and a hive of activity. Looking out of the kitchen window, she could see people setting up stalls, piled round with boxes of merchandise waiting to be displayed. Men were setting out chairs and tables that had been stacked behind the church, stocking the bar with cases of beer and wine, and laying cables around the stage. There were bursts of music from the speakers, and the odd ear-splitting shriek of feedback.

By eleven a queue of cars was crawling up the hill to the village, searching for places to park, and the square was thronging with people. Stalls offered handmade crafts and produce of all kinds from olive oil, cheeses, honey, and locally cured hams and sausages, to bread, cakes and pies, and delicious smells filled the air. A whole sheep was roasting on a spit, and a little further off an author was offering signed copies of his latest novel, a crime story set in Saint-Florent just up the coast.

All day the people came and went, and towards evening as some of the families began to leave, others arrived to take their place. The tables filled up, there was a crowd over by the bar and the servers from the local café were rushed off their feet serving light meals and drinks. Then word went round that the band had arrived, and excitement reached fever pitch.

There were eight musicians, three women and five men, playing a range of instruments including violin, sax, bass, keyboard, two guitarists, percussion and a lead male vocalist. Jessie watched their comings and goings from an open window in the house above the stage. They tested mikes and set up their instruments with short bursts of virtuoso playing, until finally they took off in a flourish of sound. No longer able to restrain herself, she ran down-stairs to join the revellers.

In no time the dancing area in front of the stage began filling up with children, closely followed by their elders. Simon emerged from the house and joined her.

'These guys are terrific!' she said, as together they skirted the stage.

'So, let's dance!'

He offered her his hand.

By now there were so many people dancing that it was hard to stay together, and Jessie eventually found herself face to face with a tall, good-looking woman, whom she'd already noticed in the village talking to Simon.

'You're Jessie!' she said in French, leaning closer to be heard. 'I'm Clemence.'

'Hi, Clemence. I've seen you around,' Jessie replied.

Clemence moved with such graceful abandon that

Jessie soon lost her inhibitions and, surrendering to the music, followed her lead.

At length the band announced they were taking a short break, and the two women paused for breath.

'Let's go and get a drink. I'm parched after all that!' Clemence said.

As they made their way through the crowd to where Douglas and Ruth were seated at a table, Simon joined them.

'Grab some more chairs. What would you like? Beer or wine?' he said.

'Beer, please,' they both replied.

He set off for the bar and Clemence and Jessie found a couple of spare chairs and brought them to the table.

'You two were really up for it!' Ruth said. 'I was tempted to join you but then Philippe and Marie-Josef appeared.'

Philippe Corsini was the village mayor and Marie-Josef his wife. They were good friends of Douglas and Ruth, who had already introduced them to Jessie with talk of getting together for dinner.

'Will they be back? Shall I get more chairs?" Clemence said.

'They're expecting friends, so they went back home,' Douglas said.

Ruth pointed up to the balcony of the Corsini house that overlooked the square.

'There they are!' she said, and waved.

They waved back, and Jessie could make out two other figures standing behind them.

'We're coming down!' Marie-Josef mouthed, and they disappeared back into the house.

A moment later they reappeared and made their way to the table, just as Simon returned with a tray of beers, some glasses and a bottle of rosé gris.

'Let me introduce our friends,' Philippe said.

One by one he turned to those seated around the table, starting with Douglas and Ruth.

'This is Paolo and Marie-Paule Savelli.'

For a moment Jessie thought she was going to faint. She had gone pale with shock, her mouth dry so that she could scarcely swallow. Next it would be her turn to be introduced, and if there'd been anywhere to run to, she'd have fled. But it was too late for that.

'And this is Jessie. She's from England. She's staying with Douglas and Ruth.'

Jessie held out her hand to Marie-Paule and gave a fleeting nod in the direction of Paolo.

'We were watching you dancing,' he said, smiling. But she'd already looked away.

'I'll help Simon find more chairs,' she said, thrusting hers towards Marie-Paule.

Then, before anyone could respond, she disappeared into the crowd.

She made a slight detour to make sure she could slip back into the house unobserved, then ran up the stairs and into her apartment, shutting the door behind her. There could be no doubt. Paolo Savelli was the same Paolo whose invitation to walk along the beach she'd accepted all those years ago. She recalled his handsome looks and gentle charm, and how she'd believed he was attracted to her when all he'd been was a decoy to lure her into the hands of her kidnappers. And now here he was with his wife, guests of the village mayor, who were good friends of the people under whose roof she was living. Call it coincidence or synchronicity, either way it was a catastrophe and she had no idea how to deal with it.

She poured herself a glass of wine and went out onto the terrace. In the distance the mass of mountains was peppered with clusters of tiny lights, and the scope owls had begun their nightly conversation, barely audible over the din from the fête. The band started up again. But she had no desire to go back and join the dancers.

Her first instinct at recognising Paolo was to avoid him at all costs. But a part of her also wanted to confront him, to witness his expression of guilt and remorse and demand justification for what he had done. The only sign he'd ever given of feelings of guilt was his gift of the pipe he'd carved for her. She recognised it as the peace-offering it was intended to be, though she'd refused to acknowledge it. But on that last evening the whole family had played together. And she recalled how the music they shared had for a brief moment united them, sweeping away enmities.

She went in search of her diary and found it in the bedroom. She turned towards the final pages.

It was the worst hour of the day, just before darkness, the time when it's hardest not to think of home. There was no one in the house, so I took my pipe out of my pocket and started to play. A few moments later I became aware Paolo was standing in the open doorway, listening. He was followed by his brothers and as soon as I saw them I stopped playing, pocketed my pipe and made myself scarce in the corner of the kitchen. They hung their jackets and leather satchels on the pegs by the door and instead of sitting down at the table like they usually do, Ermano went to the wall and took down a stringed zither-like instrument that hung there but so far I'd heard no one play. He sat down, put it across his knee and began to tune it. Paolo went to the chest and took out a flute, larger and more elaborate than mine, then he and Jesu pulled up chairs close to Ermano, and Ermano began to pick out a tune on his zither, first slowly, note by note, then in little runs. Paolo blew some notes on his flute, harmonising with him, breaking off for a moment, then picking up the tune again. Jesu produced two blocks of wood, which he started to knock together in a rhythmic beat.

Suddenly, with one accord, they took off at a brisk pace. Ermano played the main tune, whilst Paolo dipped and danced around him on the flute, and Jesu kept up a rapid rhythm with his blocks, sometimes knocking them against his hand, his elbow or even his knee.

Mama had silently entered the room. She stood watching them for a moment, swaying her broad hips to the music in a solemn dance. Then, tipping back her head to expose her strong throat, she began to sing. It was a sound so deep and thrilling, unlike any voice I'd ever heard and sent prickles down my spine. I could no longer contain myself. I picked up my pipe and began to join in, first a few notes then, as I grew more confident, descanting in and out of the tune, improvising with gleeful abandon. Never had the joy of making music felt so intoxicating.

Then suddenly all hell let loose!

She would never forget the sudden sounds of loud hailers and men shouting. Ermano and Paulo grabbed their guns and raced outside, whilst Jesu doused the light and slammed closed a shutter. Mama bolted the door then pushed Jessie into a corner, shielding her with her body while Jessie clung to her in terror. There was the sound of breaking glass as a bullet shot through an uncovered window, hitting Jesu in the chest. And then, with a splintering crash, the door fell in on its hinges and armed gendarmes crowded into the room. One of them kicked the prone body of Jesu, who didn't move. Another advanced on Mama, gun raised. He shouted at her and when she did not move, hit her with the butt of his rifle and pushed her to the door. Jessie watched as she wrenched herself free from his grasp and cried out in her strong voice, 'Flora! Bon chance, ma petite!' In the distance she could see the waiting Captain, as Mama, defiant, walked towards him, the gendarme following on behind.

'Flora! Fleur!' The name belonged to someone she'd left behind long ago. A whim of her mother's after watching a popular TV series, she'd always hated it, and had abandoned it as soon as she left home for university in favour of her second name, Jessie. But now, reading those words, she was once again that 16 year old girl, caught up in a terror as vivid as if it were yesterday and feeling as if her heart would break.

At midnight the musicians finally called it a night and were followed by a DJ, playing standard pop music, louder and more raucous than the band had been. There was no chance of sleep so she finished the bottle of wine, fetched a blanket from her bedroom and lay down on the terrace. Her eyes pricked with exhaustion and she longed for sleep. But not until the church clock across the valley struck four did the music finally cease, and she crawled wearily to bed.

She slept late and next morning when she looked out of the kitchen window, the stalls were already in full swing. She drank a coffee and ate the last of yesterday's baguette with some apricot jam, then got ready to go out. There were enough people that she could lose herself in the crowd without much fear of running into Paolo and his wife, assuming they were still here. If so, as it was Sunday, local custom suggested they'd be enjoying a good lunch with their hosts. Douglas and Ruth had several times referred to Marie-Josef as a woman renowned for her cooking, and the cheeses and charcuterie she provided were from her family bergerie.

She avoided the square and walked past the church towards the far end of the village. She was examining a stall selling handmade jewellery, when a hand on her shoulder made her turn round swiftly.

'Where did you get to last night?' Clemence said. 'We were worried about you.'

'I had a headache from all that loud music, and went home,' Jessie replied.

Clemence observed her sceptically.

'All right,' she conceded. 'I had my reasons but I don't want to tell them just now.'

'So let's go and sample some of those beignets from that stall over there. The smell's driving me crazy!'

As they ate their doughnuts, a young African girl of about fourteen joined them.

'You forgot to leave my pocket money, Mum,' she said, without smiling.

'Want one?' Clemence offered her a doughnut.

She shook her head.

'The others are waiting.'

Clemence fumbled in her small shoulder bag and produced a couple of notes, which she handed to the girl.

'Don't forget, that's supposed to last the rest of the week.'

The girl nodded and turned away.

'Teenagers!' Clemence said, as she watched her retreat into the crowd. 'She'll spend it in no time. Then she'll ask her father for more, and he'll give it to her. I don't know how we're supposed to teach them about money!'

'It's the holidays! I remember what it was like; no money and having to sponge off your friends.'

'I tell her she should get a temporary job. It's what I did, but she won't hear of it. Just wants to hang out with her mates.'

'I've not been a mother, only a stepmother.'

'Then you know how tricky it can be.'

'Worth it, though.'

Clemence sighed.

'I guess.'

Clemence offered a beignet to Jessie and took the last one herself, biting into it with a smile of appreciation.

'D'you think we need two more?'

Jessie shook her head.

'Need to save some space. There's so much more to sample,' she said, as they moved on to the next stall.

'D'you come here every summer?'

'Ever since I was married. My husband's parents are from here.'

'And you were at school with Simon in L'Île-Rousse?'

'Yes. Then we moved to Marseille. My mother's from there. But we've come back every summer since I was married, and when my parents-in-law died we inherited their house.'

'And where did you meet your husband?'

'At the university in Aix.'

They bought some charcuterie from another stall, which they ate with warm bread and a beer from a local brewer.

'I could do with some exercise after all this food.' Clemence said. 'Have you walked the paths below the village yet?'

'No, but I've been meaning to,' Jessie said.

The path, which must once have been the main route between villages, started just below Douglas and Ruth's house and followed the curve of the valley, before branching into two. One branch continued on to the village on the far side of the valley at the foot of the mountain, the other headed off to the left, where eventually it met the road then continued its climb upwards to the cemetery.

The track itself was narrow, and in places overgrown or half blocked by a fallen tree. Sometimes it descended into a hollow between stone walls and low, overhanging trees. At others it emerged into the open, running alongside wide fields with olive trees and sheep and a clear view of the mountains. Lizards and small creatures rustled in the undergrowth, and at one point as they crossed a small stream, they were surrounded by a cloud of butterflies. They spoke little, but the silence was easy, and Jessie thought how lucky she was to have made a friend so quickly and with such an immediate feeling of rapport.

It was a steep climb to the cemetery, which looked down over the village, and they were too hot and out of breath for further conversation. It was surrounded by a wall and with an entrance through an iron gate. At its centre was a windowless chapel that looked more Roman than Christian, and above the entrance two stone faces, a man and a woman, gazed outwards in wonderment at the mystery of life and death. A path led between tombs engraved with the names of local families. Some were simple, others large and imposing like tiny houses, elaborately adorned with marble angels. All were well maintained, decorated with flowers and most bore an inset cameo image of the dead person in their prime.

At the far end, a low wall separated the cemetery from the mountain that rose above it. On the other side, the land fell steeply away towards the village perched at the end of its ridge. Beyond, more mountains were half lost in a haze of blue, and to the right there was a distant glimpse of the sea.

'What a view!' Jessie exclaimed.

Clemence nodded.

'I love this place!'

It wasn't just the beauty of the setting, Jessie thought, but the feeling of serenity.

'I want to show you something,' Clemence said, after a pause.

She went over to a flat marble slab, into the head of which was carved a name and a couple of lines of verse, and above them the cameo image of a small boy of around three with dark curly hair and a solemn expression on his perfect oval face.

'This is my son, Julien,' she said, laying her hand on the stone.

Jessie was silent, too shocked to know what to say. What unimaginable feelings of anguish and grief must underly Clemence's outward calm. She reached out and covered her hand with her own.

'I don't know what to say,' she said, fighting back tears.

'It's all right,' Clemence said. 'It's ten years since he died.'

'Can you bear to tell me what happened? Not if you don't want to...'

Clemence hesitated briefly.

'One minute he was a healthy little boy, playing in his grandparents' garden. Then suddenly, without warning, he was gone. The doctor said it was an aneurism. Could have happened at any time. There was nothing to be done. We couldn't face an autopsy.'

Jessie gazed at her but did not reply. What was there to say?

'The grief doesn't go away but in a strange way I feel closer to him than ever. The memories are so alive. Especially in this place.' She smiled. 'One thing the Corsicans understand is death!'

They took the road back to the village. It was easier going, though slightly longer. They talked little, too full of emotion. But as the first houses came in sight, Jessie took Clemence's hand.

'Thank you for showing me that beautiful place where your son rests,' she said.

Clemence smiled, saying softly, 'I knew at once you were a friend.'

That evening at around six the stalls began packing up, the music ceased, and a steady stream of trucks began leaving the village. Chairs and tables were stacked up against the church wall to be collected the following day, and the bar staff were piling up crates of empty bottles, dismantling strings of overhead lights, and stuffing plastic bags of rubbish into already overflowing bins. The stage and its underpinning were to be left until the following days.

Jessie made herself supper from the various products she'd bought from stallholders earlier in the day, and took it out onto the terrace. It was a beautiful evening and she watched the mountain opposite turn apricot, then red, purple and finally grey as the light faded. A crescent moon emerged between crenellations of the mountain top and stars began to prick the velvety darkness. Except for owls and the occasional braying of a donkey, silence had reclaimed the village, and with it a feeling of calm mislaid over the past two days.

At first she wasn't sure if the light tapping she heard was real, but when it came again she realised someone was knocking at her kitchen door. She got up to open it and stepped back in amazement. Before her stood Paolo.

'Can I come in for a moment?' he said in English. 'I'd rather not run into someone on the staircase.'

For a second she did nothing, too shocked to reply. Then she stepped aside. He closed the door behind him and they stood facing one another in the kitchen.

'I watched you dancing from the Corsinis' balcony and I knew it was you, Flora. But when we were introduced, I wasn't sure if you'd recognised me. When you disappeared so quickly, I guessed you must have.'

'I'm not Flora any more. My name is Jessie. And, yes, I did. Though you're the last person I expected to meet in this village,' she added abruptly.

'Why are you no longer Flora?'

'She was someone else. I'm different now.'

'So who are you now?'

'Jessie.'

He was silent for a moment.

'Jessie,' he repeated. Then, after a pause,' Though to me you will always be Flora.'

A feeling of annoyance, mixed with a tinge of ruefulness, seized her but she quickly dismissed it.

'It must be a shock for you,' he continued.

'To see you here? That hardly describes it!'

He looked away.

'It is a small island.'

'You're here because you know the Corsinis?'

'Yes… Look, could we go somewhere and sit down for a moment?'

She hesitated, then led the way out onto the terrace.

They sat at either end of the table. Observing his awkwardness made her feel more at ease, and her sense of shock was giving way to curiosity.

'At least your English has improved,' she said lightly.

He smiled. 'I'm flattered you noticed.'

There was a pause, before he said, 'I know nothing can make up for what we did to you, the fear you must have felt, not knowing what would happen to you…' He paused, searching for the right words. 'If I could make up for any of that, I would do it… The only thing I can say is how happy it makes me to see you so well, enjoying your life… And, I guess I have no right to say it, so beautiful.'

That charm, which had deceived her the first time… she had no intention of falling for it again.

'No. You have no right. Nor do I want your apologies. I just hope your political beliefs are still strong enough to justify what you did, and let you sleep at night.'

'I don't blame you for being bitter. My views may have modified, but the things that really matter remain the same.'

'And what are those?'

He thought for a moment.

'Cultural identity, preservation of the island and its

environment in the face of greed and uncontrolled development.'

'And independence?'

'That no longer takes priority.'

There was a brief silence.

'And what brings you here to the Corsinis?' she said, reaching for more neutral ground.

'Philippe was my boss when we both worked for Crédit Agricole in Corte. We became friends. I admired his politics, radical without being excessively nationalist. I knew he'd become mayor of this village, and when I decided to stand in my own village in Niolo, I asked his advice.'

'So now you're a mayor too. Congratulations!'

'It gives you some influence over what happens locally. That can make a difference.'

'My congratulations were sincere.'

He nodded his gratitude.

'And you have a wife and family?'

'A wife and a stepson. No children of my own as yet. How about you?'

'Divorced, also with a stepdaughter. And your mother? Despite everything, I think of her with fondness.'

'My mother died eight years ago. When going through her things I found a drawing you made of her. She kept it close. When she was dying she mentioned you.'

She hesitated.

'What did she say?'

'That you had a strong spirit and would lead a good life.'

Moved by his words, Jessie said nothing.

He looked out towards the mountain.

'It's nice here. Douglas and Ruth are good people.'

'Even though they're not really Corsican!' she said, unable to resist the dig, and saw him wince.

'I'll let you finish your supper,' he said after a brief pause. 'I just didn't want to go away without speaking to you.'

Her hostility was driving him out, when there was so much more to say to each other. She wanted to ask how his life, and also the lives of his brothers, had been over the past twenty years. But she was losing her chance.

She followed him into the kitchen and at the door they paused.

'Thank you for coming,' she said. 'It was brave of you.'

'No. You have been generous, and forgiving.'

The moment was slipping away, and she tried to think of something to salvage it.

'If you're ever this way again, perhaps we could meet on more neutral ground. Have a drink or a meal.'

'I'd like that. D'you have a mobile I could call?'

She gave him the number, which he entered into his phone, and then he was gone. She stood listening to his footsteps descending the stone stairs, and then the heavy closing of the front door.

She returned to the terrace and poured herself another glass of wine. The peace she'd felt earlier had evaporated in a maelstrom of contradictory feelings. She could not deny a certain pleasure at seeing Paolo again. She'd been sixteen, little more than a child when she'd first noticed him on the beach and how handsome he was. But what, she asked herself, could possibly be gained by meeting again? They had nothing in common except the history of a crime that could only cause scandal to a man of his public standing and potentially make her the subject of gossip. Gossip which spread like wildfire in these small communities, and if their shared past were made known would expose them both to rumours of all kinds. She knew well how deep tradition still ran on the island and how memory of past injustices and humiliations endured for generations. According to Douglas, there were families in this village still at war over some perceived wrong whose origins no one could even recall. Vendetta, even now, would prevent children of warring families from marrying, cause a neighbour's olive groves to be set on fire, reducing the surrounding land to ashes, or a house bombed to a shell with no redress at law – even murder. It would take someone braver than her to risk such things. Nor did it serve any purpose to stir the embers of a trauma that had undermined her trust in others in ways she'd never truly managed to confront.

The following day she got up early and went down to the beach for a swim. The heat of the day had not yet got going, and only a handful of people were scattered across the bay. As she spread out her towel on the sand, she noticed Simon standing at the edge of the water. His back was to her and he was gazing out to sea. Not wanting to be seen, she walked over to the rocks at the end of the bay and dived in.

The sea was calm and the water almost tepid. She swam for some time and when finally she emerged from the water, she saw he had laid his towel out next to hers and he was sitting reading the newspaper.

'You went a long way out!' he said as she flopped down beside him. 'You need to watch out for the current.'

'I know. I'm not reckless.'

'I hope not. The lifeguards won't be here till the end of the month and I'm no substitute!'

She put on her sunglasses and lay back to let the sun dry her wet body. She didn't much feel like talking but didn't want to seem rude.

'You seem to have made good friends with Clemence,' he said.

'Yes. I really like her.'

'That's good. Her old friends don't come here so often.'

'Why's that?'

He shrugged. 'Left for the continent. Moved on.'

'From what I've seen, those of you who do return enjoy being reunited.'

'True. Even though our lives may have gone in different directions.'

'What about Clemence and Thierry's daughter?' she asked after a pause. 'Did they adopt her as a baby?'

He nodded. 'Before that they had a son... He died when he was three and is buried up there in the cemetery. It was a terrible tragedy. That's one of the things that ties her to this place.'

'How tragic!'

'At least they have Amal. Thierry adores her.'

And Clemence? Jessie asked herself. Aloud she said, 'It takes a lot to get over something like that!'

'If you ever do,' Simon said.

The next two days she kept to herself, driving up to the river at Bonifato, and clambering down to one of the pools tucked between its steep, tree-lined banks. She stretched out on a sun-warmed boulder and read, from time to time rousing herself to plunge into the icy water that took her breath away and left her body tingling.

Further up the track was a café, run principally for walkers. It served good, home-cooked food and as she ate lunch, she got chatting to one of the young people who ran the place. She was from Rennes in Brittany, and had developed a passion for the region.

'I'd live here all year round, if I could,' she said. 'But the café closes in September and there's no work to be had. Still, next year I'm going to give it a try.'

Jessie tried to imagine what it would be like spending the year in this remote place, with only a few passing walkers for company. To such a person it was the land-scape that mattered, the towering mountains, snow-covered throughout winter, and the river swollen in spring with melt water, cascading in an unstoppable torrent to the sea, sweeping away fallen trees and bridges in its relentless course and flooding the dried-up river bed below. Towards the end of summer storms became more frequent, with wild bursts of thunder and lightning, and rain that turned the forest paths to streams and made walking impossible for days on end. It was dangerous country if you were unprepared and at such times all you could do was huddle inside whatever refuge you'd found and watch the skies for a change in the weather. She had to admit it wasn't for her.

When she returned home, she found a note on the dining room table with a bottle of wine and some of the delicious macaroons from the local bakery. The note was from Ruth, asking her up for an apéro that evening, if she was in the mood. She was quite tired after her day at the river and would have fancied a quiet evening on her terrace but it was a couple of days now since she'd seen them and she felt it would be unfriendly to refuse.

They were seated on the balcony that faced onto the back of the church, a bottle of wine and some delicious morsels laid out in readiness. They hoped she was enjoying herself and not feeling lonely. She assured them she wasn't and described her day at the river.

'By the way, Marie-Josef and Philippe asked if you'd join them and us for dinner on Thursday,' Ruth said.

'Great. Please thank them,' Jessie said, doing her best to mask the feeling of dread that swept over her. What if the talk turned to Paolo and his wife? She'd have to find some excuse nearer the time.

'I was intrigued by your friend, Etienne,' she said, to change the subject. 'What does a man like that do in the Legion?'

Douglas laughed.

'You have a prejudiced view of soldiers! I did myself,

55

before I met him. You can ask him what he actually does. We're playing chess again tomorrow.'

When she heard the honking of the bread van next morning, she hurried downstairs. A small queue had already formed and she waited at the back of the line, careful not to push in until the regular residents had been served.

She bought her bread, walked to the café on the far side of the church and ordered coffee. The village was filling up as more people arrived from the continent. She noticed Amal, Clemence's daughter, engaged in lively conversation with a group of other young adolescents. Further off she recognised the silhouettes of Clemence and Thierry. As she observed them, Clemence broke away from him, her gaze fixed on the ground. Jessie called out to her as she walked past, and when she turned, gestured to her to join her.

'Are you ok?' Jessie said, as Clemence pulled up a chair. She had the impression she'd been crying.

'I'm fine,' she said briskly. Then added with deliberate cheerfulness, 'Why don't we go down to Calvi, have a drink at the harbour? I need to get out of this village!'

'Good idea! I'll just put the bread in the house,' Jessie said.

'I'll wait for you on the other side of the square. My car's an old VW convertible. Green.'

As they drove down the steep, winding road to the sea, Clemence put on a tape of North African jazz rock, and very soon they were singing and beating time to the rhythm. When the track finished it was followed by another, equally infectious.

'This is better,' Jessie said. 'You had me worried back there.'

'Sometimes I ask myself why I agree to come back here each year,' Clemence replied. 'It's time to go somewhere new. But for Thierry, like any true Corsican, it's still his home.'

'At least Amal looks happier now more young people have arrived.'

For a moment Clemence didn't reply.

'She has a couple of good friends but as the only black girl, it's not always easy for her.'

'Surely the young are no longer so prejudiced?'

'Maybe not the young, but some of the parents and grandparents.' She paused for a moment. 'Thierry says it's my fault. If I gave her unconditional love, she'd find her place more easily and be more confident.'

'But you love her?'

Clemence shook her head.

'I do my best but it's not enough... Sometimes I can't accept that she's here and Julien isn't. I know it's not her fault and, believe me, I hate myself for it. But the anger and grief ... they won't go away.'

Jessie was silent. She knew from her feelings for Stephanie, her stepdaughter, that love for a child who wasn't yours wasn't straightforward. For her it had grown strong with time, though it wasn't the same as the visceral love her friends professed for their children, so unequivocal they would readily sacrifice their own lives for them.

They turned into the main road that led to Calvi, and

Jessie pointed out a group of Legionnaires running along the side of the road. They wore camouflage fatigues and carried heavy backpacks, and she could see the sweat on their faces.

'What makes people sign up for a life like that?' Clemence said.

'Maybe they think it'll be an adventure.'

'Torture, more like!'

'Still, it keeps them fit!'

She thought of Etienne. Unlike Clemence the mystery of that male world intrigued her, and she remembered a wonderful French film a woman had made about some Legionnaires in Africa.

They parked the car at the edge of Calvi and walked up through the narrow tangle of pedestrian streets that ran parallel to the quay all the way to the citadel. Halfway along was a square with a handsome church built in pink stone, and tables set out around it. There was also a small market selling local cheeses and vegetables, and on three days a week fish. It was closing now as the church clock struck twelve.

They turned down a narrow alley and found themselves at the harbour, lined with cafés that looked out at the array of boats moored alongside various walkways protruding from the quayside. Some were old-fashioned sailing boats, sleekly elegant, others modern, obscenely oversized and grandiose, bristling with antennae for reception of internet and every kind of TV channel. Uniformed staff were busy cleaning their decks, but there was no sign of the owners.

'What d'you think such people find to do here?' Jessie said. 'Calvi hasn't much of a nightlife as far as I've seen,'

'And hardly a decent restaurant. Thierry thinks the owners just fly in to pick up the boat when the servants have got it ready, then sail down to Sardinia or somewhere more suited to the rich and famous.'

They found a table and ordered fruit cocktails at inflated prices, but they were on holiday and the drinks were delicious.

'I've had my moan, so tell me about your life,' Clemence said.

Jessie sipped her cocktail.

'I don't know where to start.'

'That sounds exciting!' She paused. 'Did something happen on Saturday night? You said you'd explain later.'

Jessie hesitated for a moment.

'Those friends of the Corsinis, Paolo and Marie-Paule Savelli... I recognised Paolo from years ago. Over twenty.'

'How come?' Clemence said, puzzled.

'It's a long story.'

'So tell it!'

For a moment Jessie hesitated, reluctant to revive memories so long repressed, with still the power to create fear and crippling feelings of uncertainty. Then, as succinctly as she could, she began to relate how when she was sixteen she was on holiday with a schoolfriend and her family, an English MP and his wife, and how she was mistaken for her friend, the MP's daughter, and kidnapped by members of a nationalist group, then hidden away in the mountains for three weeks before the gendarmerie broke in and rescued her.

'There was an old woman and her three sons. The youngest was Paolo.'

Clemence was silent, doing her best to take this in.

At length she said, 'And you recognised him on Saturday night?'

Jessie nodded.

'Did he know you?'

'Yesterday evening he came to see me. Before they left the village.'

'And what happened?'

'We talked a bit. I was angry. I wanted to punish him, even after all these years. Not just because of the terror but also the humiliation, for being such a naïve idiot as to think he fancied me.'

'You're sure you're not making this up?'

'I know it sounds incredible but it's true. I ought to hate him for what he did, but he and his mother were also kind to me, looked out for me. It was different with his brothers.'

Clemence was silent for a moment.

'I've only met him briefly but he seems a decent man. Certainly the Corsinis think so.' She paused. 'So, what now?'

'He took my number. We might meet up for a drink.'

Clemence looked her in the eye.

'Be careful, dearest Jessie. If what you tell me really happened, then you know what we Corsicans are capable of. In many respects the twenty-first century's hardly touched this island.'

She reached for Jessie's hand.

'What puzzles me is why you wanted to come back?'

. . .

However much she tried, Jessie couldn't stop herself from checking her phone constantly in case there was a message from Paolo. In quiet moments, seated on her terrace with a drink or watering the pots of flowers that lined its walls, which she did each evening, she asked herself what, if he did call, she would do. Over twenty years was a long time, and she knew that following her mother's death and the final petering out of her marriage, she was in a vulnerable state, hungry for the right kind of affection and ripe for adventure.

Meeting Paolo again had stirred up a host of half-forgotten, troubled feelings. The fear she'd felt for his brothers during her captivity would never leave her. Most of the time they'd ignored her, as if she didn't exist. But once or twice she'd caught Jesu, the more dangerous of the older two, watching her every movement out of the corner of his eye as she went about her chores, like a cat watching a bird while it pretends to be asleep, a look both cruel and lazy as if his contempt for her outweighed his interest. She'd detected an echo of it in Simon's friend the other day at the local café when she got up to leave, cold and impersonal, contemptuous of her both as female and as one of the presumptuous invaders, tolerated merely for the money they brought.

Clemence had warned against any further meeting with Paolo, that could not go undetected in this narrow world and would so easily be misconstrued. But despite this, she wasn't prepared just to leave things at that. Talking to him offered her the chance to get some perspective on those weeks they'd shared, and wasn't that why she'd made the decision to return here? It offered the means to lay the whole thing finally to rest.

When she'd returned home from her captivity, it had been impossible to share her experience with anyone. Those closest to her had avoided the subject, with the mistaken intention of saving her pain and helping her to forget. In any case she had no way of conveying the tangle of her emotions, that on the one hand she was intensely grateful to be safely back with her family, but on the other to hear Mama and Paolo referred to as savages deserving a lifetime in prison made her want to cry out in their defence. So she'd remained silent, locking her memories away in that suitcase, unexamined, to be 'got over' with time. And now, at last, she had the opportunity to bring them to the light of day.

Wearied by the mouse-wheel of her thoughts, she recalled Douglas' invitation to come up for a drink and meet his friend Etienne, after they'd finished their chess game. She ran a comb through her hair and climbed the stairs to their flat.

The game was already done and the three of them were seated on the terrace enjoying a glass of wine. Seeing her, Douglas and Etienne broke off their conversation and Ruth fetched another glass and a dish of olives.

'Jessie finds it hard to understand what tempts a civilised man to join the Legion,' Douglas said, referring to Etienne. 'I told her you'd explain it to her when you next met.'

Etienne's weathered face crinkled into a smile.

'I wouldn't quite put it like that,' Jessie said. 'But I see how tough the life is and I just wonder what's kept you there for so long.'

'I don't do the tough stuff those young recruits go in for,' Etienne replied. 'Wherever they're from, they have to learn French, if they don't already speak it. Some of them can't read or write. Very few already have a love of books and learning. I'm there to talk about the trouble spots they'll be sent into, and to make sure they have the skills they'll need when the time comes to move on.'

'A kind of education officer? I didn't realise the Legion cared so much about its men!'

'You're not alone,' Douglas said. 'It took Etienne years to persuade me there was anything the least beneficial about the Legion. Now I see it as a sort of international young offenders' institution, with the risks and excitement of real action thrown in, for those with nowhere better to go. And he does his best to provide some enlightenment along the way.'

Etienne laughed. 'You make me sound like a social worker.'

'In many ways that's what you are,' Ruth said. 'And a very fine job you make of it!'

'Don't kid yourself. He's still a soldier at heart,' Douglas said.

Etienne turned to Jessie. 'So what brings you to these two people?' he said, changing the subject.

She smiled at him. There was a genuineness about this man that was very attractive.

'I'm here on the recommendation of an English friend, improving my French and loving every minute of it.'

'Have you been to Corsica before?'

She hesitated briefly.

'Once on holiday with a school friend and her family. So long ago, I scarcely remember.'

'You never told us that,' Ruth said.

'It scarcely seemed worth mentioning.'

The conversation moved on to the question of supper and who was staying. In the end both Etienne and Jessie accepted the invitation. She helped Ruth bring out dishes from the oven whilst Douglas kept their glasses filled, and at length when the church clock across the valley struck midnight, Jessie got up and bid her hosts goodnight. As she climbed into bed, she thought how she couldn't remember when she'd last laughed so much or had such a pleasant evening.

She woke late the following morning. The sun was already hot, and she put up the umbrella over the table on the terrace before sitting down to breakfast. As she sipped her coffee, she picked up her mobile phone. There were two messages, one from Clemence, the other from Paolo. She felt shock like a bolt of lightning at the sight of Paolo's name, and forced herself to turn first to the message from Clemence. It asked if she was free later this morning for a visit to the market in L'Île-Rousse. Then, after some hesitation, she opened the one from Paolo.

'Hi Jessie, if you are free perhaps you could meet me for lunch at the Belle Vue Hotel in Monticello? It's a small town above L'Île-Rousse, which you can reach by the mountain road if you prefer that to the coast. I'll be there from 1p.m. mobile switched on. Paolo.'

She laid the phone on the table beside her coffee cup. Monticello was half an hour's drive via the mountain road and it was barely ten. She had time to decide whether or not she would go. If she made some excuse, she doubted she would hear from him again and that would be the end of it, undeniably the wise decision. But it was not, she knew, the one she would make.

The first thing she needed to do was to text Clemence with some credible excuse for not joining her on a trip to L'Île-Rousse. If she feigned illness, Clemence would insist on visiting her. It needed to be some prior engagement, if she could think of one. Eventually she wrote that she'd promised to help Ruth with a translation into English, which she was making for an international travel magazine. Ruth was new to translation and wanted to know how hers read, though that could be done at any time. Instead she offered to meet Clemence for a drink in the café before supper. As regards Paolo, she decided not to return his text. She would arrive at the Belle Vue Hotel at 1p.m. and take a chance on whether or not he was waiting for her.

For the next hour she distracted herself by tidying up the flat, doing some hand-washing, hanging it out to dry on the terrace, and watering the plants despite the fact the sun was at its zenith. Still in her night clothes, she ran through what she should wear. She wanted to look her best, but in the most casual way. She settled on a simple linen dress of cornflower blue, clipped up her hair into a twist, which showed off the elegance of her neck, and added the antique silver earrings her mother had given her.

The drive along the mountain road passed through woods, above which kites circled in endless search for prey, before opening out to reveal spectacular views of the sea below. Here and there a lone house perched on an outcrop of rock overlooking the coastal plain, and further on the road detoured around a small chapel for the dead, whose village lay half submerged down the hillside. Having plenty of time she stopped the car and got out to take a closer look at the chapel. It was the usual narrow, Romanesque building, built of rough-hewn stone blocks, similar to the one in her local cemetery. Above the doorway was the carved figure of a man. He was seated, with one leg crossed over the other, carefully examining the sole of his foot. There was something so vivid yet so incongruous about his placement above the lintel that she wondered what ancient myth or culture he hailed from. She'd heard that a little further north there were taller than life-size human figures, menhirs belonging to some ancient pre-Christian culture. Perhaps he was one of these, who'd somehow made it to the chapel since in this island nothing was forgotten.

Eventually she pulled up in the square of Monticello and parked the car under a plane tree. The hotel was on the far side facing the coast, with a magnificent view over the rooftops of L'Île-Rousse all the way to the sea. She entered the foyer to be greeted by a man in uniform, who asked her if she was here for lunch. She told him she'd arranged to meet someone. When he asked the name, she gave it with a slight hesitation, and he led the way to the dining room.

It was at the back of the building, with a window that

ran the length of the room and a view of the sea. There
was only a handful of diners and at once she spotted Paolo
seated at a table next to the window, reading Corse Matin.
He looked up as they approached and Jessie smiled
brightly in an attempt to mask her nervousness.

'Your guest, Monsieur Savelli,' the hotel porter said;

He pulled out a chair for her to sit down and as soon as
she had done so, picked up her napkin, shook it out of its
fold and handed it to her, before walking away.

'They're very formal here!' she remarked in English.

Paolo smiled.

'They pride themselves on their old-fashioned stan-
dards of hospitality. Not that most people care about such
things any more... I wasn't sure you'd come. You left no
message.'

'I wasn't either.'

She felt herself blushing, knowing it was a lie.

'I'm glad you did.'

He handed her the menu. She took it, avoiding his eye.

'Shall we order? The kitchen keeps rather strict hours
but we can take coffee out on the terrace without being
rushed.'

She studied the menu.

'I'll have the fish of the day, please. And a salad.'

'Me too.'

He beckoned to the waiter and gave him their order,
adding a bottle of local rosé gris. She observed him as he
did so. His thick dark hair was quite long, unlike the
shaved heads favoured by many Corsicans. But his dark
eyes were what she most recalled, eyes you could look
into without sounding their depth. He'd grown from a

lanky youth into a still slim but strongly built man of middle height, and there remained a reserve about his manner, as though waiting for the other to make the first move before offering a response.

As he gazed at her, she was overcome by intense self-consciousness. What was she doing with this man who, despite those weeks of enforced proximity in his godforsaken farmhouse, had never been other than a stranger?

'I guess you're wondering why I invited you here. I know we're little more than strangers,' he said, as though reading her thoughts.

'I do wonder.'

His English, though fluent, had a slight transatlantic lilt she didn't recall.

'I remembered how everything ended so abruptly in violence. The police breaking in and then you were gone, with no time for farewells.' He paused. 'I owe you an explanation.'

'Or perhaps an apology?'

'That would be harder. And I doubt you would accept it anyway.'

She did not reply.

'When we saw one another again in the square, I knew I had to find a way to speak to you.'

There was a further silence as the returning waiter placed an ice bucket on the table, uncorked a bottle and poured a little wine into Paolo's glass. He tasted it, nodded and the waiter filled both their glasses, before resting the bottle in the bucket.

'Tell me about your life, what you've been doing for the past twenty years,' Paolo said as soon as he'd left, then paused. 'I suppose I want to be reassured that what we did caused you no lasting damage.'

'So you can leave here, freed of guilt and with a clean conscience?'

He flinched.

'I understand your anger.'

'Actually, whatever anger I felt disappeared long ago. No, I suffered no lasting damage that I'm aware of. Strange as it may seem, I've even retained some cherished memories. Especially of your mother. What happened to her, by the way?'

'Because of her age, my mother wasn't given a custodial sentence. She died at home five years later. My eldest brother served a spell in prison. The other, Jesu, was killed in the shootout with the gendarme.'

In her mind she heard again the burst of gunfire and saw a man fall to the ground. She remembered as she was led away by one of the gendarme, looking down at his body. There was an expression of surprise on his face, as though dying was the last thing he'd expected.

'Your mother was a good woman,' she said. 'And you?'

'Two years in a young offenders' institution on the continent... So tell me about yourself.'

'There's not much to tell. I work with a group of family-court lawyers in London. I'm amicably divorced with a 14 year old stepdaughter, who still spends part of the year with me.'

'And is there another man in your life?... Perhaps you'll tell me that's none of my business.'

She smiled.

'No one else. Unlike you who are married, and newly elected mayor of your village. Quite a success!'

His face remained expressionless as he nodded his assent.

'With such standing in your community, aren't you taking a bit of a risk meeting me like this?'

'Perhaps.'

He was silent for a moment, as if gearing himself up for what he wanted to say.

'I've thought of you so many times over these past years, Jessie. '

Her name on his lips disturbed something deep inside her.

'Of course I've felt guilt over what we did, deceiving you, luring you into a trap. But it's not just that.'

He paused.

'You were for me a being from another world; beautiful, foreign, fascinating. I dreamed of how it might have been if, in other circumstances, we'd been able to get to know each other properly.' He looked away towards the window. 'You were my first love, and that, I guess, is something you don't forget. It makes no difference now but, seeing you again, I wanted to tell you.'

She was silent, fighting back tears that unexpectedly gathered behind her eyes.

The waiter appeared, placed a plate of food in front of each of them, asked if they had everything they needed, and left. For the rest of the meal they made small talk. Jessie told him how she'd come to visit Douglas and Ruth, and Paolo told her about his friendship with the Corsinis and a little about his duties as mayor. When they had finished eating, they went out onto the terrace for coffee.

For a few minutes they sat in silence, gazing out over the sea that winked and sparkled in the distance. The waiter arrived and placed a tray on the low table in front of their loungers. Jessie poured coffee then sat back in her chair. At length she broke the silence.

'When I first saw you on that beach, I thought you were the handsomest boy I'd ever seen. And being sixteen and pretty naïve, I guess I dreamed of a holiday romance... When I realised you were merely a decoy to lure me into the hands of your brothers, what I felt was more than fear and anger. It was humiliation, at my own stupidity. None of it, I realised, had been about me. I was just a pawn in your game.'

He gazed at her without interrupting.

'And seeing the way you suffered in my presence and how you tried to make it up to me by doing little things like carving that pipe, gave me a slight satisfaction of revenge. Part of me also wanted to respond to you. But I could never forgive you.'

He was silent. At length he said, 'And can you forgive me now?'

'I don't know. I don't know what I feel, except that seeing you has brought these things back and I don't know what to do about that.'

It was a while before he spoke.

'Perhaps we've talked enough for today... Maybe we can meet again? It seems our conversation's only just begun.'

'To what end?' she asked fractiously.

'To understand one another better?'

'Understand! How can we ever do that!'

'I think we can. It will give us a chance to move on with our lives.'

'You seem to have done that pretty well already!'

At once she regretted her sarcasm. It was true her captivity had coloured, inhibited even, the past twenty years, more so perhaps than she'd hitherto accepted. But an almost childish resentment held her back.

'D'you want to meet again?'

He held her gaze, so that she could not look away.

'Ok. But I think you're running a big risk.'

'That's my responsibility… I'll text you.'

She nodded.

He stood up and held out his hand.

'Thank you, Jessie. It was generous of you to come.'

The warm touch of his flesh startled her.

'You think as a result of our meeting we'll die easier?' she said brightly.

'Perhaps!' he replied, smiling.

As she drove home along the mountain road, she gazed at the passing landscape, her mind drifting in a suspended state of consciousness in which all thought was banished in a fog of confused emotion.

Back home she reached for her diary and took it out onto the terrace. She sat down and opened it up, searching for the description of her first encounter with Paolo on the beach.

· · ·

I spread out my towel and sat down on the warm sand. Behind me the town rose up in a steep curve of tangled streets. At the far end the distant outline of the mountains was blurry in the heat haze, and above the glittering water where the sky meets the sea, there were a few shreds of cloud. I felt suddenly full of life and happiness, like there was nowhere else in the world I wanted to be other than here on this beautiful beach, surrounded by blue mountains and sparkling sea.

Then I noticed someone. He was seated on a rock at the far end of the beach, just a black silhouette against the blinding light. But I knew at once it was him and my heart began beating faster. I lay back on the sand, half-closing my eyes, waiting.

After a bit I heard footsteps squeaking on the sand as someone approached. A shadow passed over my face then was gone and the footsteps ceased. I opened my eyes halfway and turned my head slightly. He was squatting on his haunches a few feet away, gazing out to sea. His skin looked very dark against his white shirt and the sun made his dark hair shine with coppery lights. His boots lay at his side, tied by the laces. He didn't move or speak. Eventually I couldn't bear the tension any longer and sat up.

'My name is Paolo. What is yours?' he said. In English!

She skipped over her description of their small talk, until she came to the part where he invited her to take a walk along the beach.

. . .

He stood up and offered his hand to help me to my feet. His skin felt warm and slightly rough, and as my face came close to his body for a moment, he smelt of the sea.

I pulled my dress on over my head, stuffed my things into my beach bag and said, 'Ok. Ready!' My voice sounded high pitched and rather silly, which made me suddenly self-conscious.

As we walked, I glanced at him. He's very handsome, with fine-drawn features and a brooding air. Byronic, my mother would have said! Though that's exaggerating, because once he glanced over at me and gave me a very sweet smile. So I began to relax. Hard to believe now how stupid I was, putting my trust in a total stranger!

She skimmed through the description of what followed. How, as they'd climbed up from the beach to where the maquis started again, they'd heard voices, and she'd been frightened when a couple of men emerged from some scrubby trees carrying rifles. Paolo had reassured her they were only hunters after chamois. But she'd sensed something was terribly wrong, and as the men started towards them, she saw it was too late to run.

She'd never forget the shock of his betrayal and what a fool she'd been. Whatever feelings Paolo claimed to have had for her, they had counted as nothing in the face of his loyalty to his brothers and their nationalist cause. And now he was mayor of his village, a respected representative of his community. The French had granted Corsica a greater measure of autonomy but not the independence they'd sought. The bombings and shootings had died down, though not ceased altogether, and the clans had mostly either disbanded or gone underground, waiting to see how events unfolded. Some had allied themselves with the mafia to ensure the flow of ready money.

But below the surface little, she sensed, had changed. Centuries of fighting off invaders had developed a violent resistance to any perceived threat from outside. It had reinforced ancient clan and familial bonds that still over-rode claims of state or conventional justice. And knowing this, what, she asked herself, was she doing agreeing to another clandestine meeting with Paolo? It would be wise not to say anything to Clemence about her lunch, nor mention any future arrangements between her and Paolo. Because, despite her better judgement, the likelihood was that if he asked her, she would meet him again.

It was Clemence who cancelled their meeting that evening. Her husband and daughter were about to return to Marseille for a while and she wanted to make them dinner. Jessie made herself a salad niçoise and went to bed early.

In the morning, finding the fridge virtually empty, she drank a quick coffee and drove down to the supermarket. At the cash desk, she picked up a copy of Corse Matin. It always amused her to catch up on local gossip. Back home she unpacked the shopping, made another coffee and took it to the terrace with the paper.

The front page was all about the outcome of an assas-sination trial taking place in Ajaccio. It involved a member of the Colonna clan, accused of murdering a state official he claimed was an informer. He had agreed to turn state evidence in order to get a more lenient sentence, preferably here in Corsica. On the last day of the trial it was the turn of the clan chief, Jacques Coppolani, to be interrogated.

'Surely you're not going to believe some Mongolian like him?' the paper quoted him as saying to the judge. 'You know full well you'll never get the truth from such a low life. He'll not confess even the little he thinks he knows because that would mean death. And since no man of honour will ever break his silence, you will never penetrate the inner workings of these organisations you claim to be criminal.'

The judge had pronounced case dismissed for lack of evidence, which just went to prove that whatever else had changed, the old networks, with their rules of loyalty and punishment, had lost little of their power.

Clemence texted Simon, asking him to meet her at a café favoured by locals up near the citadel in Calvi. She needed to make sure Jessie wouldn't see them because it was Jessie she wanted to talk about.

Knowing Simon was usually late, she settled down with a coffee and a book. Twenty minutes later he came puffing up the street and flopped down opposite her.

'Parking in this town gets worse and worse. I did the circuit three times and finally got a place in the paying bit by the station as someone left.'

'Wait till the tourists get here!'

'They're already starting.'

A girl emerged from the interior of the café to take his order - a double espresso and a croissant.

'I missed breakfast!' he said, as she left.

'How come?'

'Stayed up late talking to Etienne. I like him more and more. And he's good for Douglas too.'

'In what way?'

'When he's at the house and they get talking, Douglas is his old vivid self.' He paused. 'He doesn't admit it but he's not well. His breathing's not good and he drinks too much, which he knows is bad for his clogged-up arteries. Sometimes I catch him when he thinks he's alone, just staring into space, like he's lost that boundless energy he always had. Ruth's noticed it too.'

'Has he seen a doctor?'

'In Paris. But he won't talk about it to me.'

'That must be worrying.'

Simon shook his head, then smiled.

'Enough of that. Tell me what you wanted to see me about.'

'Jessie.'

'Really? I thought she was enjoying herself. Getting along well.'

'She is. But there's a complication.'

Simon waited for her to continue.

'You know Philippe Corsini's friends, Paolo and Marie-Paule Savelli? They were here the night of the fête.'

'Yes, I remember them. Paolo's just been elected mayor of his village in the Niolo.'

Clemence nodded.

'Jessie has told me she visited the island years ago. She

was sixteen, on holiday with the family of a school friend whose father was an MP or something important. It was at the height of all the bombings and attacks by the separatist movements fighting for independence.'

She paused. Simon remained silent.

'She was kidnapped, mistaken I believe for the MP's daughter, and held in a farmhouse in the mountains for several weeks before the police rescued her.'

'How come she's never spoken of this?' he asked, amazed.

'Would you? Something like that, that would make you into a celebrity for all the wrong reasons. She only told me because of the other thing I'm about to tell you. But first I must swear you to secrecy.'

'I can't believe this!'

'Do you swear?'

'Yes, of course.'

'Paolo Savelli was one of her kidnappers. He was only seventeen, but his two brothers were big in the local cell.'

There was a moment of silence as Simon digested this.

At length he said, 'So they met after all those years on the night of the fête. Did they recognise one another?'

She nodded.

'Have they spoken since?'

'That's just it. Paolo dropped by before he and Marie-Paule left and took her mobile number. He's going to suggest a meeting and I'm sure she will go. I'm afraid for her. If any of this gets around, it won't be good for either of them.'

'Indeed! But why does he want to see her again? And more important, why does she want to meet him?'

'That's the question.' She paused. 'Marie-Paule's family have a farm in the Niolo. I've sampled some of their excellent cheese and charcuterie with the Savellis... Her mother belongs to the Savone clan.'

Simon groaned.

'It gets worse and worse!'

'It's pretty certain Jessie knows none of this. And even if I try to explain the dangers to her, I doubt it'll make much difference if she's determined to meet Paolo.'

'Then let's hope it's just one meeting and they're not observed. To set things right between them. That's possible, don't you think?'

Clemence looked doubtful.

'I don't know... Her reaction to seeing Paolo again was shock, but also excitement.'

'You think she's attracted to him? Stockholm syndrome? Falling for your abductor.'

'She was sixteen!'

'Exactly. A vulnerable age.'

'Simon, you're enjoying this!'

'Well, it's more interesting than most village gossip.'

'And that's precisely what it mustn't become!'

'Should I talk to her?'

'Absolutely not. She mustn't know I've told you.'

'Ok. But keep me informed. She's our guest. I may need to look out for her.'

As Clemence drove home she thought about their conversation. There was something unreal about the situation, like an episode in a TV soap opera. And yet the potential danger was real. No one who hadn't been brought up on the island could understand the power of family ties, or the depth of misogyny and violence that underlay its ancient patriarchal system.

When Clemence had left, Simon ordered another coffee. Hearing about Jessie's meeting with Paolo on the beach brought back memories of his own activities at sixteen and seventeen. In autumn after the summer visitors left, he and some mates had taken to breaking into their empty houses, together with a few of the girls reckless enough to accompany them. There they could party and flirt. Occasionally they stole some small object of no great value out of a spirit of bravado, and when they left, they'd sprayed the letters FLNC onto walls or doors to mark their presence, even though none of them had any real connection with the movement.

One evening in summer he and three of his mates had gone to a club in Calvi, popular with both locals as well as foreigners. Unlike the tourists, the Corsicans were let in for free, and spent most of the evening standing at the bar with a beer, watching the girls. One of them, a lovely German blonde, was particularly striking, and his friend Herve began commenting on her looks and manner with increasing intimacy, almost as if she were already his girl-friend. As they studied her, a cool-looking foreign boy came up to the girls and asked the blonde to dance. He remembered Herve's rising fury as he took her by the hand and led her to the dance floor. For him it was as though some guy had stepped in and stolen his girl, and he wasn't having it. In no time the atmosphere grew aggressive. Herve pushed his way onto the dance floor, grabbed the boy by the arm and landed a punch on his handsome face. All hell was let loose, with chairs and bottles thrown as war between natives and tourists broke out. A moment later they found themselves strong-armed from the club and thrown ignominiously onto the street.

But anger and humiliation consumed them, and had to be assuaged. They'd been ejected without a word of apology, under the scornful eyes of moneyed foreigners, who'd continued to enjoy themselves. Some act of violence was required.

'We'll find a cow and kill it!' Herve declared, as they set off back to the village.

But that night no cows wandered the road, and as they passed a track that led to a bergerie, they turned off in search of some other beast to kill. A few metres down the track their path was blocked by Xavier, the shepherd.

'We want a lamb!' Herve announced.

'Are you preparing a feast?' Xavier asked amiably, sensing the rage that fuelled their bravado. 'I can get you one tomorrow.'

'We want it now!' Herve insisted, before Xavier saw them off with a hail of stones.

Simon could still recall that longing for violence that burned within them. Violence surrounded them on every side. They saw it in the theatrical wildness of the landscape, the savagery of its weather and its winters, above all in the bitterness of its proud, beleaguered people. Violence had been the undoing of those three young friends - Herve dead at eighteen, having committed suicide after the death of his father, Dominique who was serving eighteen years after shooting dead a police officer, and Jean-Noel who had moved to Bastia and was rumoured to be a rising member of the local mafia. Simon recalled him saying, 'Violence keeps you alive!' - though not, it seemed, for so many of the island's people. It was a drug that fuelled their pride and frustrated energies, something Jessie could never understand or know how much it was to be feared.

Three days later Jessie received another text from Paolo, inviting her to meet him in the Auberge des Cicognes, a small hotel/restaurant where the bay of Ostriconi meets the Désert des Agriates, a wild uninhabited area that went all the way up to the bay of Saint-Florent. He would be there at 11a.m. the following Thursday. She texted back saying she'd be there, and looked up the hotel on the map. Ostriconi was a wide sandy bay a few kilometres beyond L'Île-Rousse. The hotel was situated just off the road near the junction that led to Ponte Leccia and the interior of the island. The journey would take a little less than an hour by the coast road, roughly the same amount of time it would take Paolo to drive from the Niolo.

So far she'd managed to avoid the subject of Paolo with Clemence, though it lay unspoken between them. For the sake of their friendship she could no longer keep from her that she had already seen him and was planning a second meeting. She invited her for supper the following evening.

She bought fish in Calvi market, aiming to make something special and to dispel any Gallic prejudice about English inability to cook. She laid the table with candles in glass holders to keep the wind from blowing them out, made a salad to go with the fish and had a bottle of Chablis chilling in the fridge. Then she sat down to wait.

There was a tap on the kitchen door. She called 'Entrée!' and a moment later Simon appeared on the terrace, carrying a bottle of rosé.

Seeing the table laid for a guest, he hesitated.

'Sorry to intrude! It's not important. Another time.'

'It's ok ...'

But before she could finish her sentence, he'd turned away.

As he re-entered the kitchen, he ran into Clemence, who'd entered unannounced.

'Oh, it's you!'

'You thought you might muscle in on my dinner invitation?' Clemence said casually. 'Well, I guess you can stay for one drink, eh Jessie?'

She nodded at the bottle in his hand.

They went out to the terrace, where Simon poured the wine and told them about the coming music festival, Calvi on the Rocks. A couple of good bands were expected to play.

'Personally I think the whole thing's best avoided,' Clemence said. 'Except you can't because it's so loud it resounds across the entire bay! '

'When did you lose your taste for fun, Clemence?'

'It's just not my idea of fun. Anyway the music's usually rubbish,' she retorted.

'Well, a couple of the bands are good. So don't prejudice Jessie. She might enjoy it.'

He poured the rest of the rosé into their glasses, downed his and stood up.

'It's time I left you ladies to your dinner. It smells wonderful!'

The fish was delicious. Afterwards they finished off the Chablis with a strawberry tart Clemence had brought.

At length she said, 'So, have you heard from him?'

Jessie nodded.

'And seen him?'

She nodded again.

'All right, tell me.'

'We had lunch in Monticello, some fusty old hotel. He talked about the kidnapping and how sorry he was.'

'Sorry!'

'I believe he was sincere. It's clear the guilt still haunts him, however much he justifies their actions.'

'They kidnapped you, as they'd carefully planned, and held you prisoner. Whatever he says now, Jessie, his loyalties lie firmly with the cold-blooded men who'd ordered it. You were just a pawn in their game. Nothing can change that.'

'Ok. But he was only seventeen. He had to go along with his brothers.'

'Even if he felt pity for you, I doubt he regretted his part in the action. Those loyalties come first, and believe me they don't change.'

Jessie looked away. When she returned her gaze, Clemence saw the fierceness in her eyes.

'It wasn't just pity. He said I was his first love. And it's true, there is a connection between us.'

'And for you? Your first love?'

Jessie heard the sarcasm in her tone.

'Maybe love's the wrong word. But ever since that time something inside me has remained frozen, like I could never allow myself to let go.'

'And you think seeing Paolo will help you unfreeze?' Clemence shook her head. 'That's trauma, Jessie. Trauma he caused, and the only way to unlock it is to see a therapist. Not plunge back into some nightmare fantasy.'

They were both silent. Then Clemence said, 'I'm sorry to be so brutal, but at least you should know one thing. Paolo's wife is a member of the Savone family, the most powerful clan in their region. Any insult or perceived injustice to her will bring down retribution, not just on Paolo but quite possibly on you. You're already the cause of Paolo's family having spent time in prison, possibly of his mother's premature death. They don't need another reason to hate you.'

Jessie was silent. She couldn't bring herself to tell Clemence that Paolo had invited her to another meeting, and that she'd already accepted. But this one would have to be their last.

As soon as she woke in the morning, she called Pierre and arranged to go riding with him. She needed a distraction to help her through the two days before her meeting with Paolo and this was the best she could think of.

When she arrived at Pierre's field, the horses were already saddled up and Pierre seemed impatient to be off. She greeted her mare with a chopped-up carrot she'd brought with her and a quick scratch behind the ear, packed the few things for the ride into the saddle bag, and mounted.

'There's a storm coming,' he said. 'We'll be lucky if it stays in the mountains.'

This time they turned in the opposite direction from their previous journey, up a steep, stony path to the village she'd driven through on her way down. One or two people looked out from their doorways, drawn by the sound of clattering hooves on tarmac. Pierre greeted them in passing but no one looked at Jessie, as though she were invisible. The weather was sultry and overcast, with dark clouds gathering over the mountains and the occasional distant rumble of thunder.

They rode in single file till they were out of the village, then trotted the rest of the way to the ridge. There they paused to look down over Speloncato to the distant sea, still bathed in brilliant light.

'This is where in winter you loose your horses, so they can return to Belgodère?' she said.

'A bit further along. I'll show you.'

They left the road as it curved away to the left and began its descent, taking the grassy track that ran along the ridge as far as the eye could see. Already Jessie could feel her mare tensing in anticipation of a gallop.

'Ready?' Pierre called over his shoulder.

'Ready!' she replied, and with a sudden leap the horses took off at speed.

Her mare was keen and it took all her strength to keep her behind Pierre. Her hat, held on by its ribbons, was blown to the back of her head and the wind stung her face as the horses' hooves pounded over the sandy track.

Beneath her she could feel the mare's muscles as they expanded and contracted with each lengthening stride. Never had she experienced such power, or the exhilaration of such speed.

A moment later a flash of lightning lit up the mountains to their right, followed by a loud crack of thunder. In fright the horses raced even faster, until at length Pierre managed to slow his speed and she wrestled her mare into falling in beside him.

'Wow! I've never been so fast!'

'You're ok?'

'Never better!'

He pointed towards the columns of rain drifting in their direction.

'We're going to get soaked. We'd better turn back.'

She patted her mare's neck.

'They loved that! A shame we have to go back!'

They turned as the first drops of rain struck them and she could feel how the temperature had dropped.

'Have you got a waterproof in your saddlebag?' he said.

'I'm afraid I didn't think.'

'We'll take the shortest way back.'

They descended via a series of steep paths, growing slippery with rain, and avoided the village. When the rain hit them in earnest, to Jessie's relief the mare's tendency to skitter with fright at any flying debris lessened. But by the time they reached Pierre's field, she was soaked to the skin and her hair dripped into her eyes.

'Get under the shelter and dry yourself off. There's a towel hanging there. Not very clean I'm afraid, but the best I can offer,' Pierre said, dismounting. 'I'll untack the mare.'

She rubbed her hair but there was little she could do about her clothes. Her teeshirt was sticking to her like a second skin and she noticed Pierre turn his gaze away from her exposed body.

'There's nowhere to shelter except my caravan, and that's no place for a lady. But there's a restaurant just beyond Ranucci's theatre. It's not far and you'll be able to dry off there.'

She nodded. She'd have preferred his caravan, whatever its condition. But she knew that in no circumstances would he consider inviting her inside.

'I haven't paid you.'

He shook his head.

'Next time. And let's hope for better weather!'

As she walked to the car, she began to shiver. Inside, she searched for the sweatshirt she'd left there, found it and peeled off her teeshirt, using the driest part to wipe her exposed breasts. She glanced towards Pierre in case she was visible through the car window but he had his back to her, busy rubbing down the horses under the shelter.

She hesitated for a moment before pulling on her sweatshirt, wondering why she felt such an urge to expose herself to him. It wasn't because she fancied him, though he was an attractive man. It was more a desire to provoke the way he, and most of the other Corsican men she'd encountered, had of putting her off limits, as though neutralising her existence. Like when he'd sat on that rock with his back to her, never glancing over, whilst she swam in the river. But worse than that was the brief sound of laughter, not from him but from the man whose grinning face she'd glimpsed looking down on her near nakedness in the water. There was a gulf between men and women that couldn't be breached, despite at times the illusion of friendliness. In cities where men and women were accustomed to living and working side by side, friendships between them were as common as love affairs, and often more enduring. But here on this island friendship between the sexes, if contemplated at all, seemed as dangerous as love.

And what did that mean for her and Paolo? What hope was there for openness and mutual understanding? She decided not to stop at the restaurant but to drive straight home, and turned up the heating in the car.

As she crossed the ridge and finished her descent towards the coast, the rain stopped, the sun reappeared, and the temperature rose.

The morning of her second meeting with Paolo broke fine and hot. Eager not to look as if she'd made too much effort, she dressed in a well-worn batik print cotton shift, sturdy sandals for walking and her panama hat. She chose the coast road because it was quicker, though the journey would still take up to an hour if traffic through L'Île-Rousse was heavy. As Ostriconi bay opened up before her, she saw from the clock on the dashboard that she'd be early and slowed her pace.

She arrived at the hotel at 10.45 and parked the car under a tree. An eating area had been laid out next to the hotel, with tables and umbrellas and an open-air kitchen. A delicious smell of coffee and freshly baked bread greeted her, and she saw Paolo seated at one of the tables reading his usual Corse Matin. He looked up as she approached and greeted her with a smile of such simple pleasure all hostility fell away, and her suspicions vanished.

He'd waited for her before ordering and they both chose coffee and freshly baked brioches, with some of the hotel's homemade jam from the apricots in their orchard. He told her about the Désert des Agriates, on the edge of which the hotel was situated. For centuries it had been the site of the transhumance, the shepherds' yearly movement of their flocks by boat from Cap Corse for the summer grazing. You could still see the conical stone huts they'd used as shelters, he said, and suggested a walk there after breakfast. If she was up for it, they could ask the hotel for a picnic and go on to one of the beaches reachable only by foot or boat, where they could bathe.

Flowering shrubs and a host of wild plants lined the path they took through the Désert. Mostly it was smooth going, with now and then steep, rocky patches that formed sudden clefts and gulleys in the scrubland. The mixture of herbs crushed underfoot as they walked, and the flowers on the plants and bushes created a strange, heady perfume, and the only sounds were from birds and insects. The place had a pristine feel, as though untouched by human hand.

It had grown hot and from time to time they paused under a low tree for water and a short rest. Sometimes Paolo pointed out a particular bird call, or they stopped to observe some small creature scurrying through the undergrowth. But mostly they walked in a silence that felt easy and companionable. At length they arrived at a low cliff, and saw below the white sand and irresistibly clear water of a small bay.

As soon as they'd climbed down, Paolo threw off his clothes and ran into the sea. Jessie changed into her bathing suit and waded in more slowly, relishing the refreshing coolness of the water. She watched as Paolo disappeared then resurfaced with all the ease and delight of a porpoise. Not many Corsican men, it seemed, took such pleasure in swimming, except perhaps the Legionnaires for whom the beach offered a rare moment of relaxation.

They returned to the shore and lay down, a little apart, on the hot sand. Jessie put her hat over her face to keep off the sun, and when eventually she pushed it aside, she saw Paolo propped up on one elbow, gazing at her. He turned away quickly and offered her his towel to cover herself against the burning heat.

'The sun's really fierce at this time of day. You should be careful.'

'I covered myself in sun cream before I left home,' she replied, as she took the towel and draped it around her shoulders,

Their hands touched briefly in the exchange and she felt a sudden stirring of desire. His wet hair clung to his skull and the skin on his back and chest was slightly paler than the dark tan of his arms, being less used to exposure. He rubbed his hair with his hands to shake out the sea water and pulled on his teeshirt.

A little way out to sea a boat was lowering anchor, and as they watched two men and a woman dived into the water and began swimming to land.

'What a shame!' Jessie said. 'We were the only two people in the world!'

The newcomers nodded a greeting in passing, and walked towards a rocky outcrop further down the beach. One of them carried a backpack from which a couple of snorkels protruded.

'I guess they're going fishing in the rocks over there,' Paolo said.

'Will they catch anything?'

'Crabs maybe and perhaps sea urchins. They're quite a delicacy if you know how to prepare them.'

At the mention of food, she felt suddenly hungry.

'Shall we eat our picnic?'

'Just what I was thinking,' he replied.

He opened his backpack and laying down a cloth on the sand, unwrapped bread, saucisson, cheese, tomatoes and figs, and set out two beakers and two flasks, one containing water, the other wine.

'Please. Eat!'

Needing no encouragement, she tucked in. As she ate, she gazed out over the glittering sea and wondered if the semi-stranger at her side felt the same peaceful pleasure in her presence. They knew each other so little and yet there was an easy complicity in their silence.

Eventually Paolo spoke.

'Tell me about your life, Jessie. I know so little about you.'

'There's not much to tell. It hasn't been very eventful, though I've no complaints about that.'

'I guess after Corsica you weren't looking for "eventful".' She smiled.

'Perhaps that's why I married a quiet man, more of a friend than a lover. I went to law school and joined a practice focusing on family cases. Eventually husband and I went our separate ways, though we're still friends. One good thing came out of it. My stepdaughter, Stephanie, who stays with me part-time. She's fifteen.'

'And are you happy?'

'Happy! I don't really know how to answer that.'

'It's a simple question.'

She shook her head.

'You might ask someone at the end of their days, have you had a happy life? Then they might answer you. But now? … Right now I'm in the thick of it, trying to find out what I want, how to live.'

For a moment he said nothing.

'And you? Are you happy? What about your family?'

'My mother is dead, as I told you. My wife, Marie-Paule, was a young widow when I married her with a two year old son. She runs her family farm, with the part-time help of her uncle now that her parents are old and infirm. They make cheese from the milk of their goats and also a small amount of charcuterie from the special pigs we rear.'

'That must keep her very busy.'

He nodded.

'The farm has been in her family for generations. One of her brothers lives nearby and helps out whenever he can. The other lives in Bastia. It's lucky that all three of them have been able to stay on the island, as these days so many have to leave for the continent.'

'You tell me all this. But still you haven't answered my first question.'

He shrugged.

'Because I don't know the answer.'

'You see! Not such a simple question after all.'

He smiled.

'Yet it was me who asked it.'

She smiled.

'Well, at least you're a mayor.'

'Of a small village. No big deal, as you say.'

'It gives you some influence in your community, and that obviously matters to you.'

'It matters that people accept and trust in the rule of law, rather than the old ways of settling grievances.'

'And do they?'

'Some do. For others traditions must be upheld.'

She was silent for a moment.

'And if your family knew about our meeting?'

There was a brief pause before he said, 'It is a risk I'm prepared to take... My wife knows about the kidnapping. But there would be no reason to imagine we would ever meet again.'

'It is indeed a coincidence!'

'But not, I think, mere chance.'

Chance or not, she told herself, it was for them to decide what happened next.

'Perhaps it's a good thing I won't be staying for much longer.'

His expression darkened.

'But I hope we may see each other whilst you're here.'

She lay back, without replying. After the long walk and all the food and wine she'd consumed, she felt sleepy and dangerously relaxed. But to go to sleep here on the sand might seem like rejection, or worse still provocation. She resisted the impulse and sat up again.

'Perhaps we should go back.'

'If you're ready.'

He began packing up the picnic and she knelt up to help him.

When he'd stowed the remains into his backpack, she folded the cloth and handed it to him, then pulled her dress over her now dry bathing suit and stuffed her towel into her bag.

'Ready!'

The walk back to the hotel was steeper than the way down, and the afternoon had grown hotter. They spoke little, until eventually the hotel came in sight.

'Thank you for today, Paolo. It's been wonderful,' she said as they reached her car.

She wanted to tell him how much the wild land-scape, beach, picnic, and above all being with him, had meant to her, but she lacked the words. She hoped some intuition might enable him to read her feelings as they stood facing one another. For a second she wondered if he might reach out and embrace her. But he made no move and the moment passed.

'Shall we meet again?' he said after a brief pause. 'I'll understand if you'd rather not.'

'No, I'd like to. But I know it's risky. Especially for you.'

'Don't worry... Today was special for me too... I'll be in touch.'

As she drove home, she went over their parting conversation, so stilted and inadequate. Yet she couldn't allow herself to speak frankly about feelings for Paolo that were taking a dangerous turn. The excitement she'd felt at their first encounter on the beach all those years ago had been a stupid adolescent fantasy. Since her captivity feelings of anxiety had grown and those of spontaneous joy all but disappeared, as though stifled before being born. In neither her marriage nor the few, brief infidelities she'd indulged in had she experienced real satisfaction. No doubt a therapist would have put this down to unresolved trauma, but whatever the problem or its solution, one thing was clear. She and Paolo should not meet again.

The following morning, she went into Calvi to buy cheese and vegetables from the market. As she inspected one of the stalls, she became aware of someone standing beside her. She turned and saw Etienne. He was dressed in well-pressed khaki trousers, white shirt, and his close-cropped head was bare. Though not in uniform, the neatness of his appearance denoted a military man.

'Time for a coffee after your shopping?' he asked.

She accepted his offer readily.

The town was already getting busy. They took one of the last free tables in the square next to the pink church, and ordered coffee and tartines with jam.

'You're not on duty today?' she said.

'Officially I'm always on duty. This morning I had to sort out a visa problem for one of the young recruits. It gives me an excuse to visit the bookshop, one of the pleasures of coming into town.'

'You read a lot?'

He smiled.

'I also run the camp library. It's gratifying how many of the books actually get read, especially during the slow times between missions.'

'How did you meet Douglas and Ruth?' she asked, after a brief silence.

'Through Philippe, the mayor, and Marie-Josef. They invited the three of us to dinner. Douglas and I hit it off at once. I love his anarchic humour and endless curiosity. And then, of course, we share a passion for chess. And you? How do you know them?'

'A friend back in England suggested I come here, and they agreed to have me.'

'So this is your first time in Corsica?'

She hesitated a moment.

'Yes... I've fallen in love with it!'

'And you've already made friends, I hear. Simon, of course, but also Clemence Geronimi.'

'Word gets around!'

'That's the way of villages.'

'You know Clemence?'

'Not well. I know her husband a little. He comes from the village. She, I believe, is from L'Île-Rousse, but grew up in Marseille.'

'An outsider, then!'

He smiled.

'It doesn't take much to be considered so.'

She felt there was something he wasn't telling her.

'You make it sound like she's not really accepted.'

'Perhaps at first. But that changed since the death of their son and her wish for him to be buried in the cemetery above the village. Corsicans respect death above all things.'

'Is that why they're not afraid of violence?'

'Piety and violence are the outstanding characteristics of the Corsicans. Murder is wrong, but it is also the sacred duty of the wronged family to avenge any wrongs. You could say an act of vengeance is considered to be more unfortunate than sinful.'

'That sounds all too Jesuitical!'

He laughed.

'Nothing on this island is simple.'

'At least these aren't questions to trouble your young soldiers too much!'

'Fortunately our men are mainly concerned with the goings-on of their own small world. And, of course, their next mission. Everything else takes second place. Which can be hard on their women.'

Their talk turned to the island and its turbulent history, including the family of its most famous son, Napoleon. Another of its heroes, Christopher Columbus, was claimed by Calvi and celebrated by a large statue below the citadel, but the story was purely mythical according to Etienne, since Genoa among several other cities also appropriated him.

'Will you stay on when you leave the Legion?' Jessie asked at length.

'That's a question I sometimes ask myself, and I don't know the answer. My family, what's left of it, are in Rouen, not a city I feel any connection with. All my life I've gone from one place to another. The idea of settling seems rather alien.'

His frankness touched her.

'Maybe you could teach, in a university somewhere? You seem to work well with young people.'

'It's an idea, though I don't know what sort of institution would have me... I've a few more years to work it out.'

She sensed an unexpected vulnerability, a man without roots or connections, for whom, it appeared, no one waited or claimed kinship. He was also a man of intelligence, insight, and kindness – precious qualities in any human being. How, she wondered, had he gone through life without forming any lasting attachment?

The evening was warm and the sun not yet set. She decided to go to the beach for a swim, before going home for supper, and parked the car under the pines at the top of the dusty track that led down to the beach. Only a handful of people remained, among whom she spotted Clemence. She was in the process of packing up her things and leaving, but seeing Jessie she put down her stuff and waited for her. Jessie took off her dress, under which she wore her bathing suit, and together they waded into a sea coloured apricot and peacock blue by the dying sun. Lights were coming on across the bay in Calvi, and two large cormorants flew in and settled on a rock a short distance away, with no show of fear.

They swam to the end of the bay and sat side by side, gazing at the miraculous colours of the horizon. Jessie thought about Etienne's remark concerning Clemence and the death of her son. She wanted to say something about it but couldn't think of a way to broach the subject without spoiling the mood.

'If life could always be this peaceful!' Clemence said, taking her hand.

'Is something troubling you?'

Clemence sighed.

'No more than usual.'

'Tell me. I know things aren't always easy for you.'

'It's an old story. Trouble is, on this island nothing ever dies.'

'You don't have to tell me if you don't want to.'

For a moment they remained silent. Eventually Clemence said, 'When my little boy Julien died, I wanted to bury him at home in Marseille. To be near him. But we decided to bury him here. It's Thierry's home and the home of his family, and as a result people here finally accepted me.

'Thierry's mother was still alive then and he got a job as a notaire in L'Île-Rousse so we could stay and look after her. I found myself at home all day, suffocating with grief and loneliness. He tried his best, but he was away all day, and his mother was elderly and infirm. I felt as if I was losing my mind, and eventually I could endure it no longer. I told him I was going to Marseille. I still had my mother's flat. I could get back my old teaching job, and of course I'd come back to the village for the holidays. He agreed to let me go, not because he wanted to but because he knew if I stayed I might do something we'd all regret.

'A friend of mine in Marseille worked in a refuge for asylum seekers. Many of the children there were orphans, and the idea came to me of adopting one of them. I'd met a three year old little girl from Eritrea and bonded with her. At first when I put the idea to Thierry he refused. You can't get rid of your grief by replacing one child with another, he said, especially if that child's not even your own. But I persisted and he came over. When he met Amal he agreed.'

'So in a way that was a happy ending?'

'For Thierry, yes, it was. We came back to Marseille, he got a job there and formed a close, loving bond with his new daughter... For me things were more complicated.'

The last of the sun was disappearing beneath the sea and the sky darkening to purple as Jessie waited for Clemence to conclude her story.

'Whenever we returned to Corsica for the summer and met members of his family, I could feel their hostility. It was clear that they, and also some of the villagers, believed I'd abandoned my husband in his time of suffering and, worse still, my ailing mother-in-law, who died during our absence. There were even rumours of my having had another man in Marseille, which were entirely untrue.'

'And how did they react to Amal?'

'Unexpectedly well. They accepted her for Thierry's sake and because he made it clear he would tolerate no harm ever coming to her, not even an unkind word. Me, on the other hand, they did not forgive. I was once more the outsider, whose sins would be neither forgotten nor forgiven.'

'So why d'you keep coming back here every summer?'

'It's my husband's home, my child is buried here, and in many ways I love it too. Whatever hostility there may be is never expressed openly. Only by small remarks and gestures. I doubt Thierry believes it exists any more. But I know I have to watch my step.'

'But not with Simon, or Douglas and Ruth?'

'No, not with them. And a few others like them – Françoise, the doctor, for example, and the Savellis. With those people I can ignore the others, and life is bearable.'

She pointed at the gradually darkening sky.

'We'd better go back. It's getting chilly.'

'Come back to my place for supper and a glass of rosé?' Jessie said.

'A glass, but then I need to go home and make supper.'

Jessie nodded and together they swam to shore.

As they entered the house, they met Simon, running down the stairs two steps at a time.

'Where's the fire?' Clemence said as they moved aside to let him pass.

'I've just heard we've won a contract for the restoration of three murals in a castle near Pisa! I'm off to celebrate!'

'Congratulations!' they chanted.

He paused.

'The band who played at the fête are giving an open air

concert tomorrow night near L'Île-Rousee. D'you fancy going?'

'Love to,' Clemence said, and Jessie nodded. 'But forget Thierry. It's not his sort of thing.'

'Great. I'll pick you up from here. 8 o'clock,' and the front door clanged to behind him.

The following evening Jessie was dressed and ready to go by 7.30. She wasn't sure if Simon had meant Corsican time, which would be around nine and which Clemence probably shared, so settled herself on the terrace with a glass of wine and book to wait. At 8.15 Clemence arrived and ten minutes later they heard Simon descending the stairs.

'Ready?' he said, poking his head round the kitchen door.

Three of his friends were waiting by his car, two men and a young woman.

'Are we all going to get into that thing?' Clemence asked doubtfully.

The car was an old-fashioned Peugeot station wagon.

'I'll lie in the back if there's not enough room on the seat,' Giles, one of the friends, said.

'Get in! It easily takes eight, and we're only six,' Simon retorted.

They were in high spirits, with a few drinks in them already, and Jessie soon found herself caught up in their mood. It reminded her of years ago, on the way to some music festival or club to spend the night and probably most of the next day in crazy abandon. Rick, her husband, wasn't much into music or dancing, so when they got together she'd stopped going to gigs, and by the time she was on her own again ten years later such days seemed to be past.

They parked the car behind a row of others and made their way to an improvised gate, guarded by two women. They showed passes handed to them by Simon and entered. The arena was a field, where the dry grass had been trampled smooth and tables set out around the edges. On the far side a stage had been erected and roadies were busy adjusting cables and testing mikes. There was no sign yet of the band but the space was filling up rapidly and the excitement was palpable. Simon and his friends recognised several people they knew. They embraced or clapped one another on the shoulder in a euphoria of bonhomie, then commandeered a table not far from the stage just as a couple of others were preparing to sit down.

'You keep guard. We'll go and get drinks,' Simon said to Jessie, Clemence, and the young woman called Eugenie.

It was a hot night but the band's energy never flagged, and very soon people were up and dancing. Jessie kicked off her high-heeled shoes and found herself partnered with Michel, a newly qualified oceanographer from the training school near Calvi, and about to leave for Mauritius and his first job in the field. He was looking forward to it, he said during their snatched moments of conversation, but not without regret. His three years on the island had given him a sense of purpose and transformed his life. One day he hoped to return. He was handsome and a terrific dancer, and if he'd been staying, she thought, they might well have met up again. At least it would have offered some distraction from Paolo.

On the way back to the car he took her in his arms and kissed her, and for the rest of the drive back to the village she rested her head on his shoulder in a state of semi-slumber, dreaming of a simple life full of friends such as Michel.

When she woke the next morning, the day was already hot, so she erected the umbrella and took her coffee and freshly squeezed orange juice out onto the terrace. A pair of brightly coloured bee-eaters flew in from the valley, swooping among the plants in pursuit of insects that buzzed around the blue flowers of the plumbago. At that moment her phone pinged with a message.

For a while she left it lying next to her coffee cup on the stained marble of the table. Instinct told her it was Paolo, and as long as she resisted the urge to pick it up, things between them would remain the same and no harm would come. The alternative was to answer him and allow whatever was brewing to take its course.

She went to the end of the terrace and leaned on the low parapet. Three kites hovered over the valley, two adults, the third a newly fledged chick in the process of losing its outsized fluff for the sleek plumage of its parents. She watched as first one, then the other plunged to the ground in pursuit of prey, whilst the chick made a lunge for the safety of a nearby tree. She turned back to the table and picked up her phone.

'If you can, meet me in the square at Feliceto, Tuesday 12p.m. P.'

Feliceto was a village she'd driven through on the road to Spelancato on her way to ride with Pierre. Tuesday was the following day. She stared at the message for a long moment, then typed, 'I'll be there,' and pressed send.

She drove slowly along the winding road that followed the steep curve of the hillside above the coast. At Cateri she turned inland, until eventually she came to a sign announcing the village of Feliceto. Unlike other villages huddled above or below the road, this one followed the highway, with a row of one-storey cottages that ended in a café, a small grocery shop, and at length the central square. Opposite the square were two large, gated villas, each separated by a meadow, and gardens that descended the hillside towards vineyards and far away, the sea.

She parked the car beside the square, which was shaded by plane trees with benches on two sides, and in one corner a couple of swings and a slide for children. On the far side was an imposing building, which she took to be the town hall, and beside it a smaller building, over whose doorway an ornate sign said 'Domaine de Vanelli'. Paolo was seated under a tree, reading a book.

He looked up as she approached and greeted her with a smile that destroyed all misgivings. She sat down beside him.

'I'm glad you came,' he said.

'I nearly didn't.'

'I believe you. That's why I'm glad.'

She laughed, reminded of the ease she felt in his presence.

'D'you want a drink or coffee before we go?'

'Where are we going?'

'There's a house where I sometimes stay, just up past the village. I brought a picnic.'

'That's fine. I'll wait for the picnic.'

'My car's parked across the road. We can leave yours here, if that's ok.'

'So, no chance of my making a quick getaway!'

For a moment he looked puzzled, then smiled as he recognised a joke.

His car was parked outside one of the villas, and as they drove off, she asked what connection he had with this place.

'Gianni Vanelli is an old friend of mine. He owns the vineyard here.'

'So people here know you? Is that a good idea?'

He shook his head.

'He also has a house near L'Île-Rousse, where he lives with his family and usually we meet there. He comes here for the vineyard. It's his passion.'

'Is that his house over there?'

She pointed at the villas. He nodded.

'It's been in his family for generations, but his wife and children prefer to live in town.'

'A Corsican bourgeoisie! I was beginning to think that didn't exist.'

'But not like on the continent. Here they keep their connection to the land.'

He took a turning to the right past a ruined water mill,

and drove for a few hundred metres up a forested track until they came to a small, single-storey cottage with a roof of thatched reeds, surrounded by a small, well-kept garden. He opened the boot of the car, brought out a couple of shopping bags, and led the way up the path to the house. Jessie followed, smelling the lavender, rosemary, thyme and basil that stood in pots on either side of the door. Further off there was a vegetable patch where tomatoes and beans were already ripening, and next to that a bed for flowers: cistus with their big yellow and white blossoms, bright orange day lilies, daisies of various sizes and colours, and the blue viola native to the island.

'Who takes care of all this?' she said.

'Madame Bonelli. She lives in the village and doesn't have a garden, so she comes here.'

'It's beautiful.'

'It's my sanctuary, though I come all too rarely.'

'Is that something you need? A sanctuary?'

'I guess we all do.'

She followed him into the neat kitchen, where he deposited the shopping bags and began unpacking them. He laid out on the kitchen table bread, cheese, eggs, salami, tomatoes, salad, an apple tart, and wine.

'Another feast!' she exclaimed.

'Are you hungry?'

'Very!'

'Will you wash the salad and I'll do the rest? '

She picked up the lettuce and took it to the sink, whilst he went into the neighbouring living room and threw open the shutters onto a terrace, shaded by a thick vine with a view over the village to the vineyard below.

They ate lunch at the table there and afterwards, as they finished their wine, talked about the changes brought by the breakup of the old independence movements at the turn of the new century, some of whom had gone underground or formed links with the mafia.

'In former times we considered ourselves partisans, and did what we had to for the sake of the cause. I'm not excusing all our actions, but we had nothing to do with organised crime. Now people have come in from the mainland, whose aim is just to make money.'

He spoke calmly, but there was an underlying note of bitterness as he described how over the years concessions had been won, but still little had changed. Traditions remained strong, and his job as mayor was both to respect them, whilst fighting off corruption. Especially when it came in the name of investment and future prosperity. It was a tricky line to hold.

As he spoke, he ran his hand through his hair in a gesture she recalled from the time of her imprisonment. Then it had been in response to the bullying of his older brothers, who mostly excluded him from their conversation. He was the youngest but he was also different from them. His mother understood this and did her best to protect him, but she was long dead. Now, despite a wife and family, Jessie sensed something of that isolation had never been assuaged, especially in such a tight community where consciousness of belonging was chief among its blessings.

She reached forward and took his hand, feeling the slightly rough warmth of his skin against hers. He turned his face to her and held her gaze. For a moment they remained still. Then he stood up, raised her to her feet and led her back into the house.

Inside the bedroom he stood a little apart from her, hesitant. She went to the bed, lay down, and opened her arms. As he lay down beside her, she drew him close, closing her eyes, and felt his mouth press against hers. Her lips parted, and a flood of desire swept through her, pleasure so long withheld it felt entirely new, filling her with warmth and delight.

It was dusk when she woke from a deep sleep. For a moment she couldn't think where she was, then opened her eyes to see Paolo. He was gazing at her, as if memorising every detail of her face and body. She gave him a smile full of love, and pulled up the sheet to cover them both.

'You're so beautiful!' he said.

'Don't look too closely. I'm no longer that 16 year old girl!'

He stroked the hair from her forehead. 'You are a woman, and far lovelier than I could have imagined.' He kissed her neck and breast.

She pressed her face against his chest, then pulled away and sat up. 'The sun's almost down. Shouldn't you be getting back?'

'I hate to think about time.'

'Won't they be waiting for you?'

He sighed and sat up too.

She got up from the bed and began gathering her clothes that were scattered on the floor. He watched her dress, and when she turned away, chided her laughingly for hiding from him. In contrast he was easy in his nakedness, his body slim and muscular from daily walking in the hills with his flock, and his skin naturally dark, even the parts not tanned by the sun. She felt, as she observed him, a deep unconscious bond, almost as with some long-lost kin. And yet he was virtually a stranger.

'Where do we go from here?' she said, as she looked into the mirror and ran a comb through her hair.

He came towards her and rested his hands on her shoulders.

'I don't know... I've been reckless and selfish.'

'Now you say so! When you knew the danger you were putting us both in!'

She turned to him in a flash of anger. It was the same as the first time he'd betrayed her on the beach all those years ago. Once more he'd lured her into a trap, seducing her with his caring attentions, yet refusing to take account of the consequences.

'You have every right to blame me,' he said gently. 'Believe me, nothing is more important to me than your wellbeing. No harm will ever come to you here.'

Her anger subsided at the thought of losing him once more.

'Even if you could make sure of that, you're much more at risk than me. I have no desire to tear your life apart, Paolo... I love you and I know there's no future for us.'

There it was, the word 'love'. In the rush of emotion, she had used it and it was too late to retract. He walked over to the window.

'Would you rather we ended it, here and now?'

His voice was quiet and expressionless.

'No!' She paused. 'What I feel for you, is the feeling that's always eluded me. But I will return home in a short while and you will go on living with the consequences. I can't be responsible for you suffering.'

He went to her and took her hands, holding them tight.

'That responsibility is mine alone.'

She bent her head to hide the tears that gathered in her eyes. He cupped her face between his hands and, raising it, kissed them away.

'From the first time I saw you, you opened my eyes. You were from a different world, and I've often asked myself whether what you brought with you can have a place here on this island.'

'And what do you reply?'

He was silent for a moment.

'Meeting you again, I think we are not ready. Perhaps not until we've become like everywhere else.'

'A big price to pay!'

There was nothing more to say. The intensity between them had led to the fulfilment of sexual desire and a closeness that had always eluded her. But it resulted in a dead end. For the first time in a long while she felt truly alive, but ahead she saw no shared future.

It was nine when she arrived home. She entered the house making as little noise as possible and went out onto the terrace. As she lay back in her chair, her thoughts drifted, unfocused. She heard the calls of the night birds and smelled the mingled scents of herbs and flowers from the valley as the day's heat retreated. She raised her eyes to the myriad stars of the milky way, neither asleep nor awake but in a state of profound relaxation, in which all thoughts of past and future were obliterated by the vividness of a present in which she knew herself loved.

In the morning she woke refreshed and full of energy, and went down to the beach for an early swim. The sea was calm and clouds had not yet gathered over the mountains. Clemence was already spread out on the sand, reading a book. Jessie sat down beside her and took off her dress, under which she wore her bikini.

'What have you been doing with yourself? I haven't seen you for days,' Clemence said, turning to face her.

'Two, in fact. I've been mainly at home, answering emails and clearing up the mess in my little flat. And you?'

'Seeing if Philippe can help us sort out a dispute with a neighbour. A piece of land attached to my mother-in-law's house, has been appropriated by him. Now he's claiming she bequeathed it to him before she died, because years ago it had once belonged to his family. Of course, neither he nor we have any document to prove it.'

'That sounds tricky.'

'Worse than that. Land causes feuds that can go on for generations. People setting fire to a neighbour's olive groves or vines, or worse.' She sighed. 'Sometimes I wonder why we don't just sell up and stay in Marseille. But to Thierry this is still his home.'

'He's a lawyer. Can't he deal with it?'

'That's just the problem. For him to get involved, it would mean war.'

Jessie was silent. There seemed no answer to the problem.

'Shall we go into the water?' she said eventually.

They got up and went to the sea.

After a long swim, they dried themselves and wandered down the beach to a café, which had just opened up for the season. They ordered beers and sat down at a table on the veranda, where there was shade from the already fierce sun.

'You're looking blooming,' Clemence said, gazing at Jessie. 'It's not hard to guess why, but better not go around declaring it.'

Jessie blushed. 'Is it that obvious?'

Clemence nodded, then added on a more serious note, 'You must be careful. I've heard talk.'

'What have you heard?' Jessie asked, alarmed.

'Oh, just a rumour. But that's how things start.'

'Is the village talking?'

Clemence shook her head.

'Not yet. But someone suggested you might have been involved in a kidnapping many years ago. I don't think they've yet made a connection to Paolo.'

'How on earth did they find out?'

'People here have long memories, and it's a small world.'

'So where did you hear about it?'

'Simon heard it from the father of one of his mates, who used to be in the FLNC.'

'And did he mention Paolo?'

'I don't think so. But you need to be extra careful. And warn Paolo when you're next in touch.'

Jessie felt cold, despite the heat of the day. Nowhere, it appeared, was safe from prying eyes and ears. She would see Paolo again, if only to warn him. And that must be the last time.

'Simon may talk to you. I thought you'd best be warned.'

'My God! And do Douglas and Ruth know?'

'Only him, so far.'

But that was little comfort. If word got out about her kidnap, it wouldn't take long for someone to connect her to Paolo.

That evening as she ate supper on her terrace, there was a knock at the kitchen door. She went inside to open it and Simon was standing there.

'D'you mind if I come in?'

She stood aside for him to enter, took an extra glass from the cupboard and led the way back onto the terrace. She poured him some wine and pushed the glass towards him.

'I know why you're here,' she said, as they sat down. 'Clemence told me about the rumour of my having been kidnapped over twenty years ago.'

'So it's true?'

'It is.'

'So why did you come back, Jessie? Surely not for revenge?'

She gave a brief laugh. 'What revenge could I possibly take?' She paused. 'I wanted to see the island again, with grown-up eyes.'

'And has it brought back memories? Bad ones?'

She shook her head.

'It wasn't like that. More that some part of me stopped growing since then. As if in some way I'd got stuck. I needed to see the place again.'

He was silent for a moment.

'The eighties and nineties were troubled times on the island. Some people will find it hard to believe you haven't come here to stir up old wounds.'

'That's why I didn't tell anyone... But now it's more complicated.'

He looked puzzled, and she wondered if she should continue. But it was too late now. She had to trust him, because she needed advice.

'Paolo Corsini, Philippe and Marie-Josef Savelli's friend, is one of the family who held me in captivity. We recognised each other at the fête.'

For a moment Simon was silent.

'Meeting again like that is an extraordinary coincidence. But it happened, and what worries me now is that if people get to know about the kidnap, how long before someone makes the connection to Paolo?'

'His family are known members of the FLNC. His brother, I believe, is still active. It's a small world.'

He waited but she said nothing.

'So have you seen Paolo or talked to him since?' he said at length.

'We've talked. It was impossible not to once we'd recognised each other.'

'I understand.' He paused. 'But it's important things go no further. Not just Paolo's but also Marie-Paule's family are a strong political force in the region. People with links to what are now considered terrorist crimes are still liable to prosecution. Any threat to them would not be taken lightly.'

'I understand that. But Paolo's people were punished at the time, and I've no intention of bringing further shame on either family.'

He shook his head.

'I'm afraid you don't understand, Jessie. Punishment by the law has nothing to do with shame. Perceived wrongs must be avenged personally, and ways of doing so haven't changed. When I'm driving in the car and I hear a motorbike tailing me close, I'm afraid. I might be a target, and whoever it is has mistaken me for someone else. All it takes is a passing shot. The bike moves on and you're dead. No witnesses and no one the wiser. Believe me, any contact between you must cease.'

His words frightened her, and for a moment she was silent.

'One thing I beg you, Simon. Please don't tell Douglas and Ruth about my having been kidnapped. I'd hate them to feel I'd betrayed them by hiding something like that from them.'

'I'll do my best. But you should have told them.'

'I know. But I never thought anyone would find out. And if it hadn't been for the fête, they wouldn't have!'

Her voice trembled.

'I understand,' he said more gently. 'What matters now is to draw a line under whatever contact you've had with Paolo. Forget you ever saw him.'

Simon climbed the stairs slowly to the family apartment. The situation with Jessie was more serious than he'd thought, and she had no real understanding of the dangers she courted. And Paolo? What could he be thinking of to risk such possible catastrophe? Perhaps having worked in the bank at L'Île-Rousse then being elected mayor, he considered himself a man of the twenty-first century, despite having lived all his life in the Niolo, and now raising a family there. He wondered whether he should speak to Douglas. His knowledge of people was profound, and his advice always sound. But on reflection he decided against it. The fewer who knew about this, the better, and the main need was to keep it that way.

When Jessie went to bed that night, she was full of fear and grief. Once more she was trapped in a conflict that wasn't of her making and which she could do nothing about. Not since those weeks of captivity had she felt such helplessness. She'd come to the island looking to bury whatever harmful memories remained, not to be driven out once more and by the very people who'd done her wrong in the first place. To them she was simply one of a long line of invaders, whose only aim was to amuse or enrich themselves at their expense, and, in her case, most likely to exact some sort of revenge.

At length she fell asleep and woke in the morning, knowing she must see Paolo one last time and settle things between them. Then she would return home, and with luck whatever rumours existed would quietly die down. It grieved her deeply but it was the only solution.

Each day she waited for him to contact her in a state of tension she was barely able to control. She followed a routine of beach in the morning for a swim, returning around lunchtime via a visit to the supermarket, reading and a short siesta during the heat of the day, then an early evening drink with Clemence and sometimes Simon, though she found herself doing her best to avoid him. Usually they met in the local café, and once in one of the expensive ones situated around the harbour in Calvi. The bright lights and buzz of people gave her a flavour of the nightlife she might in other times have sought.

On another evening she invited Douglas, Ruth and Etienne down to her terrace for supper. She cooked lasagne, followed by salad and a strawberry tart, and Douglas regaled them with his endless fund of stories and adventures.

'I've noticed it's always Mary, not Jesus, on the high altar,' Jessie said, as they served themselves the last of the wine. 'Why is that?'

Douglas and Etienne looked at each other.

'You're the scholar,' Douglas said. 'You answer.'

'The mother of God was introduced from abroad in the late medieval period into a society dedicated to male heroism, where women were both subordinated and feared. She gained ground only very slowly, mainly due to the Franciscans, who created her cult, and she was associated with love and forgiveness. Unlike most things Corsican, she was wholly disassociated from war, and by the seventeenth century she'd conquered the population. A century later the new-born state under Pasquale Paoli made her their acknowledged queen.'

'Why were women, if they had such a secondary place, also feared?'

'They were credited with having special powers – such as voceratrice or even mazzere, associated with death.'

'I've heard of the voceratrice, women who mourn the dead and cry lamentation. But who were the mazzere?'

'When we first came to this village over forty years ago there was still an old woman who was held to be a mazzera,' Douglas said. 'They're night hunters, people who dream of death and who predict it. They can be women or men, but mostly women.'

'What do they hunt?'

'Animals, especially wild boar. They hunt at night, and when they've killed their prey, they look into its face and see the features of someone they know. This presages that person's imminent death. They don't cause death. They see and predict it.'

'And you saw such a woman? How did you know what she was?'

'She was well known – and much feared. There were rumours she'd grown up in this house.'

Jessie shuddered.

'Are you trying to scare me?'

'There are photographs I can show you of self-confessed mazzere,' Douglas continued. 'All have an extraordinary intensity of gaze, eyes that are piercing and blank at the same time.'

'One of the words for death in Corsican is "falcina", meaning "she who carries the scythe", Etienne said. 'Some think this reflects an ancient belief in the primeval Mother Goddess, giver and taker of life, a divinity revered in the megalithic areas of Europe. We have our own megaliths here, and there is archaeological evidence of her cult in Corsica.'

'So much for the subjugation of women!' Ruth said.

'So is Mary also an echo of this goddess?'

'Not according to the Catholic Church!' Ruth replied, laughing.

They talked of where the megaliths could be found, and Douglas got out a map. It had been both an entertaining and informative evening. But as she lay in bed, Jessie was filled with disturbing thoughts that found their way into dreams that were strange and vaguely menacing.

On the fifth morning she received a text from Paolo, asking her to meet him again at the cottage in Feliceto on the following day around noon, and suggesting she once more leave her car in the village and walk up to the house. At the prospect of seeing him her heart beat faster and her spirits soared.

The day was hot and slightly overcast. As she climbed the track to the cottage, clouds were gathering over the mountains and there were distant rumbles of thunder, though that was no guarantee of a storm. At the top of the track she turned the corner to see Paolo, waiting for her in the open doorway of the cottage. She ran into his arms, abandoning caution in the joy of reunion. Without preliminaries he led her to the bedroom, they took off their clothes, and lay down together. As he pressed her naked body into his, she felt only a sense of utter rightness, one being as it was always meant to be.

Later, as the afternoon wore on, they lay watching the light change through the open window, then made love again and drifted for a while into sleep. They'd talked little - personal things only, with few references to their daily lives. They inhabited different worlds and this moment of intimacy was their only meeting point.

Around five o'clock there came a gentle knocking at the front door. Paolo got up, pulled on jeans and teeshirt, and went to answer it. Jessie lay listening to the low sound of men's voices, and in a couple of minutes Paolo returned.

'You need to get dressed, Jessie,'

She heard the urgency in his voice.

'What's happened?' she said, getting up from the bed.

'That was my friend Michel Vanelli. Someone has noticed your hire car parked in the village. They reported it to the mairie as abandoned.'

'I don't understand. My car's not abandoned.'

'I guess they did it to find out who's hired it. The mairie would have checked with the hire company.'

'Would they give out my name?'

He nodded.

'We'll go to Michel at his vineyard. He will return to your car with you, make it look like you've been visiting him to buy wine.'

'This is crazy.'

'I know. Let's go.'

They got into his car and drove down to the Vanelli Domaine, avoiding the village. A long track led through acres of well-tended vines till they reached a house and outbuildings built around a wide courtyard, one of which served as a reception area. Chickens pecked happily among tufts of grass and a goat, tethered under a shade tree, eyed them suspiciously. Michel Vanelli was waiting for them in the main outbuilding. It was filled with huge wine vats and racks and boxes of bottles, with a table and glasses laid out for sampling wines.

'Welcome!' he said, smiling at Jessie. Then added, 'Now you're here you might as well sample some wine. What would you like to try?'

'I leave the choice to you,' she replied, charmed by his warmth.

Whilst he went in search of bottles, she glanced around her with interest, imagining for a moment they were here just for a tasting.

He returned with three bottles, two of white, one of rosé.

'Which would you like to try first?'

'The white, I think.'

She pointed to one of the bottles.

'This one is fresh with a good note of fruit and a hint of the maquis,' he said, uncorking it and pouring a small amount into a glass for her and one for Paolo.

He placed a small spitting bowl and a glass of water on the table, but having taken a sip and liking it, she downed the rest.

'I know you're not supposed to swallow, but it's delicious!'

Michel smiled.

'Better not swallow all three, if you're driving home.'

'I think you should be going,' Paolo interjected. 'This is a good time because there'll still be people about who'll see you and can witness you buying wine.'

'Of course,' Michel said. 'I'll pack up a box for you, Jessie, and accompany you back to your car.'

Whilst he went off in search of a box and the bottles, Paolo turned to her.

'Michel will drive you back to your car. I'll wait here till he returns.'

'And when will I see you again?'

'I need to find out who's interested in you and why.' He took her hand. 'I'm so sorry about all this! I'll be in touch as soon as I can.'

'Are you afraid?'

He shook his head. 'Dearest, Jessie! I just need to make sure no one's following you.'

Michel returned with a box of wine. They followed him out to the courtyard to where his car was parked. Jessie got into the passenger seat and they set off up the track. Paolo watched them go.

When she reached home, she found a parking place in the square and carried her box of wine to the house. An old man seated on a bench nodded his head in approval as she passed.

'Vanelli!' he said, quoting the name on the box. 'You believe in quality, Madame.'

'So they tell me,' she replied, smiling, and entered the house.

Inside the kitchen, she put the box down on the marble settle and stretched out her back to recover from the weight. There was a note on the settle, inviting her up for an apéro with Douglas and Ruth around eight - if that was good for her, no need to reply. She wasn't feeling much like socialising but it was a couple of days since she'd seen them and she didn't want to appear unfriendly.

Douglas poured wine as he regaled them with the latest scandal from Calvi, concerning a wealthy widow whose son he'd several times consulted as a notary.

'An intruder broke into the old woman's house, and suspecting no one she knew would arrive unannounced at such a late hour, she went to the door armed with the poker. The man attempted to force his way in so, before he could lay hands on her, she struck him a blow on the head and laid him out cold. Now she's accusing her son of having hired an assassin because he's after her money. It's well known he's deeply in debt. He's due in court the following week.' Douglas chuckled in delight. 'I doubt he'll be available for consultations for a while!'

He poured himself another glass, and got up.

'Dear Jessie, you'll have to excuse me. I've an article to finish for a French travel magazine. Routine stuff but it pays the bills.'

They said goodnight, and he went off to his study. Left

alone with Ruth, the conversation faltered. After a pause, Ruth asked if she was beginning to get bored with village life. If so, she could well understand it. For a moment Jessie wondered if she'd been invited expressly so Ruth could talk to her.

'On the contrary. I feel I'm just settling in.'

'I'm glad. I know you recently lost your mother. I wouldn't want you to feel you're without friends.'

Jessie found herself blushing.

'I've rarely felt so welcome. And I'm constantly discovering new things. Today I went to the Vanelli Domaine at Feliceto and bought some excellent wine. It's the first time I've visited a working vineyard.'

'You chose well. Michel Vanelli's a good man and makes fine wine. Did someone advise you or did you just come upon him by chance?'

She shook her head.

'I noticed their shop in the square at Feliceto as I drove through on my way to Olmi-Capella to ride. I decided to pay it a visit next time I was passing. The shop was empty but Michel Vanelli happened to come in while I was there, and invited me down to the vineyard for a tasting. Now I intend to visit others!'

'Then you'll have plenty to talk about with Douglas. He has strong views on local wine growers, and is always happy to share them,' Ruth said.

Fine smells of supper were wafting from the kitchen. Jessie stood up and placed her empty glass on the table.

'Thanks for the wine. I'd best leave you to your supper. Next time I hope you'll come to me!'

There was no obvious reason for the unease she felt

during her conversation with Ruth, but it refused to leave her. She sensed an undercurrent of suspicion, too vague to put a finger on, but which meant she'd become the subject of gossip and conjecture. Her fear was that word might have gone round she'd once been the victim of a kidnapping. Any hint of that would inevitably make her return seem suspicious, and sooner or later someone might make the connection to Paolo.

For the first time she began seriously to question the wisdom of staying on. What, for example, would be the reaction of Douglas and Ruth if it became known she'd been seeing Paolo? They lived here and however much Douglas made fun of some of his neighbours' wilder antics, these people were his friends and neighbours and his loyalty must primarily be to them. In London if you became the subject of gossip, people got bored pretty quickly and moved on to something else. But in small communities like this nothing was ever forgotten or forgiven, and the only way out was to leave.

She made herself a supper from whatever remained in the fridge and took it out onto the terrace. The night was calm and the sky clear now and full of stars. She felt restless, alert to every sound: the distant murmur of human voices, the incessant calls of scope owls, and small rustlings amongst the plants as the gecko went about his nightly hunt for moths.

Then another sound intervened, a gentle tapping at the door onto the staircase. For a moment she thought it might be Paolo but not, surely, so soon after they'd parted. Perhaps if she ignored it, whoever it was would go away.

It came again, this time more insistent. Reluctantly she got up and went inside.

It took a moment for her to recognise Ermano, Paolo's eldest brother. His face was thinner and more lined than she recalled, his hair cut short and greying, accentuating the uneven roundness of his skull. His expression was cold and set, just as she remembered it, and the fear it inspired was like a physical blow. She gazed at him, sixteen years old once more, frozen into silence.

'Are you going to invite me in?' he said, and without waiting moved past her into the kitchen. His voice was slightly hoarse and he spoke French, though hitherto she'd only ever heard him speak Corsican. 'Better close the door. We don't want to attract attention.'

She backed away as he walked past her into the next room. He looked around him then pulled out one of the chairs beside the table, gesturing her to sit down.

'Nice place,' he said. 'Nice family who live here, so I'm told.'

She sat down and he followed suit.

'My coming here must be a shock for you, Flora, after so long. I only learned a couple of days ago you had returned to the island.'

Rage at the arrogance of his manner mingled with her fear.

'My name is no longer Flora, and I doubt this is a social visit to welcome me back to the island.'

'No longer Flora? You want to wipe out the past?'

His smile was far from friendly and she made no reply.

'You're right, of course,' he continued after a pause. 'The question is, why did you come back?'

'Is that any business of yours?'

'It is when you set up secret meetings with my family. Are you out for revenge? Though it's a bit late for that. Here things have moved on.'

'So, what's my visiting this village to you?'

'If you come as a tourist, one of our many summer visitors, nothing at all. But if you come looking for us, with vengeance in your heart, that's another thing.'

'What revenge could I possibly take? You've already served time for kidnapping. Though that, no doubt, didn't harm your reputation! Crimes committed in the name of a freedom fighter seldom do.'

He grinned mirthlessly.

'You think you can insult me, calling me a fighter for freedom?'

She did not reply, and there was a moment of silence as each considered the other.

'What do you want with my brother?'

Another shock of fear ran through her.

'I want nothing. We recognised one another at the village fête. Pure chance. That's all.'

'You're lying. You have been meeting. More than once, I believe.'

She was about to deny it, but felt it was safer to remain silent.

'If this is how you take your revenge, it is not only you who will be harmed,' Ermano said.

'Should I take that as a warning?'

He observed her, expressionless.

'In our world, honour and respect are highly valued. My brother is a family man, the respected head of his village. Whatever we did to you in the past was done for political, not personal reasons. We looked after you and took care no harm came to you. Now you return filled with anger and ill will, to dishonour him and his wife and child in your petty quest for revenge.'

She fixed him with her gaze.

'You know nothing about me, or my motives. You say you did me no harm. A 16 year old girl, held in captivity by people with whom she didn't even share a language and with no idea if she would ever get out alive? You know nothing of the harm you did me, because to you your crime meant nothing. It was done for your cause! When I came to this island, I had no idea I would meet you or your brother again, nor would I have wished to. Paolo and I met by accident at the fête. But talking with him has helped me understand a little better what happened to me then, which hardly makes me a criminal!'

The rush with which her words poured out made her breathless. Apart from the love that had so unexpectedly sprung up between them, and that she prayed he knew nothing of, everything she said was true.

'You are clever with your words. But they change nothing. My warning is clear. One of my brothers is already dead because of you. Stay away from the other.'

The dead brother, she recalled, was Jesu, killed when they stormed the farm to rescue her. And now Ermano was blaming her for his death at the hands of the gendarme! But for the moment she let that go.

'You want to know why I came here? Because, despite everything, I grew to love this place, your mother especially and her kindness to me. But that, of course, means nothing to you.'

Ermano tensed visibly. Her casual reference to his mother, as if the two of them had enjoyed some special relationship, enraged him. It was as though she were claiming the right to an intimacy only family, not the intruder she was, could know.

'You are a stranger here and always will be. Perhaps you should remember that!'

He stood up and his look of hatred mingled with contempt froze her blood. Then he turned on his heel and the kitchen door closed behind him.

She sat where she was, listening to his footsteps descend the stairs. She heard the street door shut but remained still until all sound of his presence had faded. Her heart was pounding and after a few moments she got up and began pacing from kitchen to dining room and back again in a turmoil of fear and rage that made her want to beat her head against the wall. Ermano was as unlike Paolo as it was possible to be. Hard-wired into his convictions, he shared nothing of Paolo's openness, imagination or kindness. Nevertheless, it was his world Paolo had chosen to inhabit, and to confirm Ermano as an enemy was as dangerous for Paolo as it was for her. It was a long time that night before she fell into a fitful sleep.

The following day she threw herself into the routine she'd established of beach and a swim first thing, a quick shop, followed by lunch and a siesta. When in the afternoon, Simon knocked on her door and asked if she fancied to go into Calvi for an evening aperitif, she pleaded a headache from too much sun. He was sympathetic but she knew she couldn't hide away forever. At least it appeared that no one in the house had remarked Ermano's visit.

In the early evening she took the ancient path from the bottom of the village and walked up to the cemetery. The sun was still hot and the path grew ever steeper, winding its way around rocks and tree roots. When she reached the gate she was out of breath, and paused to take a drink of the water she'd had the foresight to bring with her.

Entering the cemetery, she saw a couple of women tending their graves. They were removing dead flowers and cutting away the tendrils of climbing plants that threatened to overtake the headstones. She nodded to them in passing and walked on to the far end, where Clemence's young son was buried.

She laid a sprig of wild eglantine on his stone, then sat down on the low wall that separated the graves from the mountain side. The declining sun filled the land with light, turning the rooftops below golden. Over to the right a thin band of cloud had formed, separating sea from sky, and soon it would swallow up the dying sun. As on her previous visit, she was filled with a deep feeling of peace, as tension and fear gave way to an emptiness into which light flowed.

That night she slept better, and in the morning got up early and drove to the beach, hoping to meet Clemence. However unwise it might be, she needed someone to talk to.

The beach was almost empty. She spread out her towel on the sand and looked around her. Clemence was nowhere to be seen, neither on the beach nor, as far as she could make out, in the water. She put on her straw hat and lay down with her book, Sooner or later she would no doubt turn up.

After a few minutes a shadow fell over her and she looked up from her reading. The figure silhouetted against the sun was not Clemence, but a man.

'D'you mind if I sit by you for a moment?' he said.

She sat up, put on her sunglasses, and recognised Etienne. He was wearing a teeshirt and swimming trunks, and carrying a small backpack over one shoulder that no doubt contained his clothes. She took in his tanned body, undiminished by age no doubt due to his military lifestyle.

'I'm sorry to disturb you,' he said. 'You looked so absorbed in that book. But I didn't want to leave before saying hello.'

'On the contrary. I'm happy to be disturbed. My book isn't that gripping.'

She smiled at him and indicated the patch of sand beside her. He sat down.

'I've not seen you here before?'

'No. I'm not usually free until the evening. Today I've a rare morning off.'

For a moment they sat in silence, gazing out to sea. She felt a growing desire to confide in him, someone who understood the island and its ways as well as anyone, whilst remaining an outsider.

She hesitated.

Then said, 'D'you mind if I ask you something personal?... I mean about me.'

He turned to face her.

'Please! Go ahead.'

She paused a moment longer, not sure where to begin.

'A little over twenty years ago, I was kidnapped by Corsican nationalists and held prisoner in the mountains for three weeks,' she said in English. It felt easier to express herself in her native language, which she knew he spoke fluently.

He was listening intently, but made no response.

'I know it sounds unreal, but it did happen.' She paused. 'What's even more extraordinary is that recently I've re-met two of my kidnappers.'

'Here? In the village?' he said, following her use of English.

She nodded.

'There were three brothers and their mother in the farm where I was held captive. She and the youngest treated me kindly. The other brothers showed me nothing but contempt, and I was terrified of them.'

'So which two have you re-met?'

'The youngest brother and the eldest.'

'The two extremes.'

'You could put it like that.'

He looked out to sea, for a moment, then turned back to face her.

'May I ask how this meeting came about?'

'With the youngest brother it was pure accident, a chance in a million. I don't want to go into details.'

She paused, wondering if she dared tell him of

their subsequent meetings. But if she held back, he wouldn't be able to give her the advice she sorely needed.

'We arranged to meet secretly. It was important for both of us. Him because he'd always felt guilty about what they did to me, me because I'm trying to understand, after so many years, how this whole thing has impacted on my life.'

'And has it helped you?'

'Maybe, but at a cost.' She hesitated. 'For the first time in my life I've fallen in love. I mean really in love.'

'And him?' he said, after a pause.

'Him too, it seems.'

For a while he remained silent.

'This island is a strange place,' he said at length. 'Passions here run deep, more so than anywhere else I know. Perhaps after those three weeks of captivity you have some idea of this.'

She nodded.

'On the surface you may believe you've more in common with these people than what divides you. But you'd be wrong. The ancient ties of blood and honour, often in the guise of politics, persist. As do the vendettas that follow their transgression. I have seen time and again how someone can be welcomed as a foreigner, but only as far as their position as a visitor is accepted and understood.'

'I know that what I've done flouts the rules they live by. If I didn't already, his brother made it abundantly clear.'

'He himself is in a more dangerous position than you.

You can return home, as you did before. For him, this is home.'

Jessie put her head in her hands, her fingers briefly shutting out the light. Etienne had told her nothing she didn't already know, but to hear it said in her own language from his measured voice, made it impossible to ignore.

'You can get on the next plane or ferry out of here. He must stay and bear the consequences.'

For a moment she remained silent.

'It's like the reverse of the first time, when I was kidnapped. He is now my prisoner, and I hold his fate in my hands,' she said at length.

He nodded.

'If, as you say, he truly loves you, he is not going to betray you a second time, whatever the cost to himself.'

She turned to look at him.

'Thank you for being honest. I've been trying to persuade myself I can remain passive. See how things turn out, because I can't bear the thought of never seeing him again. But that's not possible.'

'No, Jessie. If you care for this man, it is not.'

Tears welled up in her eyes. The thought of losing Paolo was too hard to contemplate. But she had asked for the truth, and Etienne had confirmed what in her heart she already knew.

He stood up. 'I need to get back to my duties... I hope I haven't upset you by being so frank. You'll have to decide what's best for you. And if I can help, or offer any advice, you know where to reach me.'

'Thank you,' was all she managed to say.

She did not watch him walk away, but fixed her gaze on the open sea. He had said to do what was best for her. But what that really meant was what was best for Paolo. Whatever happened, they could not part without a final meeting. But it must be arranged with the utmost secrecy. No one, not even Clemence, must know of it. The question was, how to contact him and then how to find a way of meeting beyond the reach of every prying eye.

She got up and walked into the sea. Despite its tepid warmth, she shuddered as the waves lapped around her belly, and plunged into the water. Then, with a brisk crawl, she set out for the yellow buoys that marked the safety limits of the bay.

As she drove home, she thought about the people she'd come to regard as friends. It was crucial not to arouse their curiosity or to be seen to do anything out of the ordinary. Clemence, especially, had so far been in her confidence, so she must continue from time to time to speak about Paolo. And Simon had already asked about her plans - how long she would stay and what she wanted to do with her remaining days or weeks. She knew that each summer Douglas and Ruth expected other members of their family and though they'd be reluctant to push her out, they'd no doubt soon have need of her flat.

But the most pressing need was how to contact Paolo. She had his mobile number but a call to that would be too easily traced. She racked her brains to think of some way she could send a message to call her that he would understand, perhaps sent from another phone. Perhaps she could get hold of Simon's phone without his knowing. She'd noticed he often left it charging on the table in the upstairs living room. She might find a moment when no one was there to call him. It would be hard but not impossible. The more she thought about it, the more it seemed the only safe way to contact him.

For two days she waited in anticipation of a call, but none came. She went about her usual routine, including a walk with Clemence across the valley to the foothills of Montegrosso, and an evening drink in Calvi with Simon and a couple of his friends from Paris, who were staying in the town. By the third day she decided she must find an opportunity to get hold of Simon's phone. She would take a bottle up to Douglas and Ruth for an early aperitif on the off-chance she might find it there.

Meanwhile she took out her map of the island and spread it out on the terrace table. She found the Niolo region, and on an impulse put the name into her mobile phone. To her surprise it came up with some photos. They showed a high, wild landscape, part of the central spine of the island, with only a single road winding through it. There was something familiar about one or two of these scenes, and after a moment she realised with a shock of recognition how they resembled the view from the farm. A vivid memory returned to her - gazing out of her window at that landscape, hour after despairing hour, feeling as though she was caught in a time warp without past or future, only an endless, featureless present in which no one either knew or cared about her existence. Perhaps the memory of that feeling was why she'd never tried to discover the exact location of the farm. But thinking of it now, why would Paolo and his brothers ever have left the place where they'd been born and lived their entire lives? It seemed absurd she'd never thought of this before.

She went in search of her teenage diary and found it in a drawer in the bedroom. She turned over the pages until she came to the passage she was looking for.

This Sunday when Mama returned from Mass, she took off her shawl and hung it on a peg near the door as usual, then opened a drawer in the sideboard and carefully replaced her prayer book and rosary. I was about to run to her, when I saw Ermano and Jesu entering the doorway, accompanied by two other men. They were older than the brothers, also dressed in dark Sunday suits and black berets. Their faces were weather beaten and their hands, like Ermano's, were calloused from work. But the respectful way everyone treated them made me think they weren't just neighbours.

Mama fetched a bottle of wine and some glasses and placed them on the table, together with a plate of sliced salami and a bowl of olives. Ermano propped his rifle against his chair and Jesu and the four other men sat down. Paolo didn't join them but sat further off. I noticed how he stroked the silky ears of his dog and the quiet way she received his caress.

The older of the two strangers did most of the talking. He sat in his chair, stiff and upright, and spoke in short, rapid sentences in a rasping though not loud voice, as if accustomed to giving orders. He had a military manner like a soldier, which seemed at odds with his rather peasant appearance. Ermano and Jesu listened to him attentively, and I thought how the movement must

be like a secret, underground army, with cells like little regiments
scattered through the mountains and the discipline of soldiers.

She paused in her reading, recalling again the awful
tension in the room and the fear she'd felt in the presence
of these men. She was their prisoner and their talk,
though she did not understand it, almost certainly
involved her. They held her fate in their hands, yet it was
as if for them she didn't really exist. Only Mama and
Paolo saw her as a human being with feelings like theirs.
More than twenty years had passed since that time, and a
lot had changed. But those people who'd supported the
movement and were ready to fight for it, were still there.
And it was they who had elected Paolo to represent them.

The reality of this discovery should have confirmed, if
that were needed, the need to keep away. Instead she
found herself filled with a spirit of rebellion, a growing
curiosity to see the place again. The idea was crazy, but
still it would not let her go.

At seven o'clock she knocked on Douglas and Ruth's
sitting room door, armed with a bottle of chilled rosé gris
from Douglas' favourite vineyard. Ruth's voice called out
to enter. They were seated on the terrace, with Simon and
one of the friends she'd met in Calvi. She placed the bottle
on the table and sat down in an empty chair, doing her
best to mask her nervousness. The conversation was as
animated as usual, with Douglas in full flow.

After a while, the talk turned to a walk along the GR20 that Simon's friend was contemplating. Jessie offered to fetch her ordnance survey maps from downstairs so they could follow his route more exactly. She got up and as she re-entered the sitting room, caught sight of Simon's phone lying on the sideboard in the process of being charged. She paused and glanced behind her towards the doors to the terrace. The voices were as loud as ever, and the four of them appeared to be absorbed in conversation. This was her chance, the only one she might get, and she must seize it.

She reached into her pocket for her own phone and checked Paolo's number, then without disconnecting the charger she picked up Simon's. She knew his code because they'd already joked that using their own birth dates might not be very secure, but at least meant they could remember them. Her fingers trembled as she keyed in the numbers, waited for a connection, then started to form Paolo's number. In her haste she made a mistake and had to start again. She needed to be brief so decided simply to ask him to call her asap. She had just written the first words of her message when she felt a hand on her shoulder, and a low voice said,

'Don't do it, Jessie.'

She turned rapidly and found herself face to face with Simon.

He reached out, took the phone from her hand and deleted the words she had written, then slipped it into his pocket. Her cheeks flamed with embarrassment. She opened her mouth to speak but could think of nothing to say. Without a word, she turned to the door and fled downstairs.

In her own apartment she paced around in an anguish of embarrassment and humiliation. She couldn't face going back upstairs, but it would look odd if she simply disappeared without a word. She could pretend she'd been delayed, maybe by a phone call from home, then offer the maps to whoever still wanted to consult them, make some excuse and leave. She picked up the maps and with a supreme effort of will climbed the stairs once more. At the door to Douglas and Ruth's sitting room she paused, ran a hand through her disordered hair, took three deep breaths, then moved on to the terrace.

'Ah, here she is!' Douglas exclaimed. 'We were wondering if you'd got a better offer and decided to go out on the town.'

'No. Sorry. I got a phone call from home... I've brought the maps, if anyone wants to look at them.'

She laid them on the table, studiously avoiding Simon's eye.

'Thanks,' Pierre, the friend, said. 'Mine are back at the hostel. Let me show you where I'll be going.'

He spread them out and Ruth and Douglas leaned over to take a closer look, Douglas saying he'd long lost any interest in mountain walking, but admired anyone else's enthusiasm for it. Simon poured himself another drink, declaring he'd already had this journey explained to him ad nauseam, and sat back in his chair.

Jessie looked on, pretending some interest as Pierre traced his route through the mountains. As soon as she deemed enough time had passed, she thanked Ruth and

Douglas for their hospitality and saying she needed to make a return call to England, descended the stairs to her flat.

She sat on the terrace in the darkness, thinking about what it meant that Simon had discovered her using his phone to call Paolo. It was unlikely he would say anything to anyone, but that channel of communication was now closed. Which left only one way, even if that was too risky to be considered.

Simon accompanied his friend Pierre to his car. As Pierre drove off down the hill in the direction of the coast, he turned away from the village and walked up the hill along the road that led to the cemetery. The road still gave off a gentle warmth from the heat of the day, and the sky was full of stars. From time to time a comet shot across his vision, to lose itself once more in darkness. After a few metres the street lamps gave out but a luminescent glow came from the sea over to his left, and from time to time he heard a scuffling and glimpsed the white hide of a cow foraging in the undergrowth.

At a curve in the road he paused and leaned his elbows on the low stone wall, gazing down at the distant sea. The situation with Jessie was becoming critical. It was clear that despite her time in captivity, she had little idea of the dangers she was running, especially for Paolo. He knew Paolo a little, having met him at the Savellis a few times and once for a beer in the local café. He was a decent, gentle man, and something of an idealist. He lacked the typical Corsican machismo, due perhaps to being the youngest son of a strong, protective mother, for whom he'd cared devotedly during her dying days. It was this difference, he believed, that had encouraged Philippe to champion him to run for mayor. He spoke of him as a man with a vision for the future, free from the taint of violence associated with so many of his fellows. All this was threatened if his relationship with Jessie were to become known.

As for Jessie, he'd come to think of her as a friend, and as such to feel a certain responsibility for her welfare. He admired her courage and lack of bitterness regarding her kidnappers. Rather than condemning them as savages on whom she wanted only revenge, she sought to know their island and their culture better. It wasn't hard to see how she could be drawn to Paolo. But those around him would never understand this. To them she was only the outsider, who would bring them harm. He wasn't sure how far things had gone, but an adulterous relationship would be an intolerable betrayal, an insult to family and community that could not be borne.

The situation was critical, and yet he had no idea what to do about it. He'd already caught her in the act of messaging Paolo, and having failed she'd no doubt seek out some other way to contact him. He would do his best to watch out for her, but she was resourceful and determined, and he was no match for a woman emboldened by love.

Jessie lay awake, unable to sleep. In a part of her mind untouched by reason a plan was forming. If Paolo was unable to contact her, and she felt sure something must be preventing him, the only solution was to go to him. She had located his village on the map and had a good idea where his farm lay. Looking at the photos on the internet had, despite the risks, awakened a pressing curiosity to see the place again. Quite possibly she'd recognise certain landmarks. The idea aroused as much excitement as dread.

The question was how, when she got there, to find Paolo without arousing attention. One thing she knew was that despite being mayor, he was also a shepherd. He'd told her that last day at the cottage when they lay in bed together after making love, how his best times were out on the hills with his dog and his flock of goats, just like when he was a boy. She'd be careful not to go near the farm itself, or the village. She would walk into the hills that surrounded it, listening for the sound of goat bells, and perhaps they might lead her to him. It was a wild gamble but it was worth a try.

The next morning she got up just as the sun was appearing over the mountain, dressed, made herself a sandwich to take on her journey, picked up a bottle of water and her map of the Niolo region, and set off along the inland road to L'Île-Rousse. From there she'd follow the coast as far as the turn-off to Ponte Leccia, and after that she'd have to consult the map.

There was little traffic at this hour except the odd farm truck, and it was still early when she reached the main crossroads, where the road turned off to the Niolo valley.

It twisted and turned through deep gorges, between rocky slopes, then up into the wooded foothills of mountains on whose jagged peaks the snow still lingered. Here and there appeared patches of open pasture where a herd of sheep or goats, and occasionally the slightly built Corsican cattle grazed, and now and then an abandoned shepherd's hut with its conical roof huddled into the hillside.

She was nearing Paolo's village and pulled up to consult the map. It was sufficiently detailed to mark the existence of farm dwellings, and there were only two in the rough vicinity of the village. She made a guess which one might be Paolo's on the basis of a patch of cleared land indicated, that followed the slope behind the house to meet the foothills of the mountain.

As she drew nearer fragments of memory jolted into consciousness. Her last vision of the farmhouse had been flashing lights, the terror and chaos of armed men bursting into the house, the sound of shouting and gunfire, and a man falling. Mama had held her tight against her strong body to keep her from harm, as Paolo ran outside, arms in the air, only to be shoved aside by Ermano. For a moment her resolve weakened, but with an effort of will she pushed such thoughts aside.

She turned off the main road and parked the car at the edge of a steep, rutted track, slipped her phone into her pocket, locked her backpack into the boot of the car, and set off towards a stony bank of low trees that bordered the pasture. Halfway up, she caught the distant sound of sheep or goat bells, and as she reached the bank she could see between the trees a herd of animals grazing on the herbs and low bushes of the pasture. It was clear now from their long coats and horned heads that they were goats and not sheep.

She took the path that circuited the field and then, from a distance, came a sound that alerted every cell in her body. It was the sound of a pipe, an ancient melody that made her heart beat faster, Paolo's pipe she felt sure, for no one could play as he did. She recalled the simple one he'd made for her, which he'd said could be her voice since she shared no spoken language with her captors. She'd only ever achieved competence, but when he played his very soul sang forth.

She moved into the trees, where she had a good view of the pasture but was hidden from view. In the distance she could make out a figure she was sure was him, seated on a rock overlooking the grazing animals, a large dog lying on the ground beside him. As she watched, he paused his playing and rested the pipe on his knees. Her first instinct was to break cover and run to him. But the need to stay hidden made her pause. She recalled the moment of her capture, the sounds of movement in the nearby bushes that had alarmed her, which Paolo had said were only chamois. Then the men with their rifles bursting from the trees and racing towards them. It was a moment she'd relive time and again in dreams. And now, by some circuitous quirk of fate, it was she who was hiding in the trees.

She followed the line of cover as far as she could to get closer to him. From there she had a better view of the land below, even a distant glimpse of the farmhouse, and could keep an eye out for signs of activity. He was now only metres away and facing in the opposite direction.

Searching for a way to attract his attention, she put her fingers to her lips and gave a thin, piercing whistle. A bird in the tree above flew off with an indignant clatter of wings. The dog sat up and with a single bark turned in the direction of the sound. For a moment Paolo didn't react, then he looked round to see where the dog was pointing. Jessie stepped forward to the edge of the trees. She saw his body stiffen as if in disbelief. Then he climbed down from his rock and walked swiftly towards her, the dog following closely on his heels.

As he approached, he gave a soft command to his dog to lie down on guard.

'Jessie! How in God's name did you find this place?'

They moved together into the shelter of the trees.

'I took a chance, and then I heard you playing. I couldn't mistake it for anyone else. It was as if you were calling to me.'

He seized both her hands and pulled her close.

'This isn't a safe place for you.'

'I've been careful. I just had to see you once more before I leave.'

'I've tried to call you, leave you a message. My brother watches me, day and night. I couldn't risk putting you in danger.'

'He came to see me.'

'God forbid! When?'

'A few nights ago.'

Paolo shook his head in anger.

'He threatened you?'

'Not openly.'

'He still sees himself as head of the family, holding our honour in his hands… He will never change!'

'And he's not alone!'

'If you mean me ….'

'No! You have always been different.'

'I despise such antique notions of honour and revenge. But this is still where I belong.'

'And where you are trying to bring about change! Isn't that why you became mayor?'

'Perhaps. But I claim little credit for much improvement so far.'

She recalled the ruthless dedication of the men who'd seized and held her captive in this very place. Twenty years would not be enough to eradicate their fervour or desire for autonomy. And Paolo was one of them, however different he might seem.

'He will never again harm you, Jessie. I promise.'

'I'm not afraid of Ermano. But I know my presence threatens you. I'm leaving soon.'

He did not reply.

'We live in different worlds. And that can't be changed.'

'You are the first woman I ever loved,' he said, barely audible. 'I will love you all my life.'

She took his face between her hands and, looking deep into his eyes, was about to speak when the dog sat up and whined. They both turned to see what was disturbing him.

Beyond the trees in the far distance a woman was climbing the hill towards them. In her hands she carried a small bundle, wrapped in a white cloth.

'It's Marie-Paule!' Paolo said. 'I left the house early. She's bringing my breakfast.'

'Go to her. I'll wait here.'

She backed into the trees as the dog ran forward to meet his mistress and Paolo followed after.

She watched as they greeted one another. Marie-Paule handed him the white bundle and reached up to kiss him on the lips. They exchanged a few words in an easy, affectionate way, then she turned to walk back the way she had come. A little further on, she looked back to wave at him, then was lost to sight over the curve of the hill.

In that brief moment of familiarity between two people who knew and cared for one another, Jessie knew she had witnessed a relationship rooted deep in ties of family and inheritance. It was something she would never know, nor in truth desired. But one thing she understood. It would outlast any passion she and Paolo might feel for one another, and remain strong until the end of their lives.

He waited a few moments then walked back to the trees where she was waiting. He sensed at once her withdrawal, and in response made no move towards her.

'I should be going,' she said. 'Before the day wears on.'

He nodded, dumb with grief.

'If I were to come with you, I should be no good to you,' he said after a pause. 'And you would soon tire of me.'

She shook her head.

'No! But I know you would feel lost in my world, and that's something neither of us could endure.'

He held her gaze, but said no more. If she didn't leave

now, she would lose her resolve. She stepped forward and embraced him with all her strength, burying her face in his shoulder. He held her tight, and as she felt the beating of his heart, she heard him murmur, 'Mia Flora! Sempre bellisima!'

With the last of her strength, she pulled away.

'Go back to your rock. Play your pipe. Then I can hear you calling to me as I go.'

She watched him walk away with his long, loose stride, then climb the rock and pick up his pipe. On her way back through the trees the sound accompanied her, growing gradually fainter as the distance between them widened.

At length she reached the rutted track at the edge of the wood. The sound of the pipe was now barely audible. Steeling herself, she moved out from the shelter of the trees and walked briskly on towards where she had left her car, just past the next bend where the track met the road. She turned the corner and was searching for the key in her pocket, when a man stepped out from behind the car. He had a rifle suspended from one shoulder, and with a shock of fear she recognised Ermano.

'I'll hand it to you, Madame Jessie. You've got some nerve,' he said as he came up to her.

She stood, frozen to the spot.

'What do you want?' she said roughly.

'I should ask the same of you. What are you doing on our land?'

Despite her terror, she stood her ground.

'This land where you kept me prisoner twenty years ago?'

'I doubt a desire to revisit the past is what brings you here.'

She felt a wild desire to smash her fists into his mocking face.

'You're quite wrong. That's exactly what brings me here.'

He shook his head.

'You came in pursuit of my brother.'

'If so, I wish him no harm. I've too much respect for him and for his family.'

Ermano put his hand on his rifle, though he kept it on his shoulder.

'Respect!' He spat on the ground. 'What would you know of that?'

She moved closer to the car and was about to open the door, when he took a step forward, trapping her against the vehicle.

'If I ever see you here, or anywhere near my brother again, we shall not only be talking. Take this as a final warning.'

His face loomed over hers, so close she had to lower her gaze. She tried to push him away, but he did not move. Then suddenly, as if from nowhere, a figure hurled himself at Ermano, knocking him to the ground. She watched stunned, as Paolo pressed down with all his weight onto his prone brother.

'Get in the car, Jessie!' He wasn't strong enough to hold him long. 'Go, and don't stop till you get back to your village!'

. . .

She drove the twisting road towards Ponte Leccio, doing her best to keep her speed under control, filled with rage and terror. When at length she reached the turn off to the coast road, the adrenalin subsided a little and she began to breathe more freely. Stronger even than her hatred for Ermano was fear for Paolo. It was a terrible thing she'd done, going to their farm only to be discovered by his murderous brother, then abandoning him to his fate. His defence of her would add fuel to their already bitter conflict and put him in even greater danger. Ermano was a fanatic, one of the Movement's most loyal activists, and loyalty to the cause took precedence even over brother-hood. As mayor, Paolo might be in the public eye, but that only exposed him further to danger from those whose respect for traditional ways set them against any attempt to bring about change.

Then there was the reputation of his wife's family. How would they react if Jessie's presence were to become known? Would they take sides with Ermano against their son-in-law? And how far would they be prepared to take their revenge? She had witnessed a moment of tenderness between husband and wife that had brought home to her the strength of the bonds that united them. Perhaps they were strong enough to withstand the consequences of her own foolish recklessness. She could only pray that they were.

But despite such feelings of guilt and regret, images of her meetings with Paolo continued to plague her. At first it had seemed strange that two people from different worlds, divided by trauma, should experience such deep connection that felt as natural as breathing. In her wildest dreams she'd imagined them leaving here and making a life together. But to go where? It was now clearer than ever that transplanting either into the other's world would annihilate that connection, though that made the inevitability of losing him no easier to bear. Meeting him again had opened up some part of her that for so long had been locked away. With him, it was as if she had come to life after being half asleep. And now she had put him in mortal danger.

Seeing the farm had also brought back memories of the woman she'd learned to call Mama, and the grief she'd felt at the moment of their separation. Mama had been her fierce protector, and despite the nightmare of her captivity, through her she'd received a healing glimpse of unconditional maternal love. It did not rival the love she shared with her own mother, who in some ways was more of a close friend than a mother. But it was a gift she had retained.

Ermano climbed the path that led steeply upwards from the village to the cemetery, his hunting rifle over his shoulder. It was the hottest time of day, siesta time, and the cemetery was empty. A small windowless chapel dominated the cluster of small tombs with their white, domed roofs like beehives that surrounded it. Above its doorway two figures, a man and a woman, gazed out at the world with open mouths and blankly staring faces.

Ermano pushed open the heavy wooden door and entered the chapel. The interior was plain, lit only from the open doorway that rose up almost the height of the building. The altar at the far end was covered with a white, embroidered cloth and above it stood a statue of Mary. She was dressed in her traditional blue robe, her head covered in a white cloth, but she held no baby in her arms and her expression was severe. This was not the Mother of Jesus, meek and mild, but some matriarchal deity from a forgotten era, goddess of just retribution, stern commander of reverence whose memory had never been erased.

Ermano placed his gun on the floor before him as though it were an offering, and knelt down in front of the altar. He didn't bow his head in prayer but gazed intently up at the statue in silent quest of her forbidding gaze. For several minutes he remained there, until at length he stood up, shouldering his rifle.

As he turned to go, he saw a figure silhouetted in the doorway. For a moment he couldn't make out who it was, then as the man entered the chapel, he recognised Stefano, the brother of Paolo's wife.

'You bring a rifle into the chapel!' Stefano declared.

Ermano didn't reply, but the tension in his body betrayed the anger that was eating him up.

'We need to talk,' Stefano said.

'Here?'

'Here's as good as anywhere.'

Ermano sat down truculently on the end of a pew and Stefano took a seat on the other side of the aisle.

'You had a fight with Paolo. What's going on?'

'He's no longer one of us. He's become a politician, who betrays his community.'

'He may wish to change things faster than some would like. That doesn't mean he betrays us.'

'Hah!' Ermano shook his head in disgust. 'You know nothing! He will drag you and your family into the dirt, and you'll just stand by and do nothing!'

'What are you saying?'

'You'll find out soon enough!'

He stood up. Stefano stood too, barring his way.

'Tell me what's going on!'

'He's making a whore of your sister. He is humiliating your family!' Ermano spat out.

He picked up his rifle and made to push past Stefano, but Stefano stood firm.

'You call my sister a whore? We're not done yet!'

He laid a hard, restraining hand on Ermano's arm.

'If you're prepared to ignore this, I swear I will not!' Ermano cried, struggling to free himself. But Stefano was younger and stronger.

Ermano reached for his gun.

'You raise a weapon in this place of worship?'

'Get out of my way!'

Stefano made another grab for him, and he twisted away. As he did so there was the sound of a shot, and Ermano slumped to the ground.

The following day Jessie went up to Douglas and Ruth to discuss a date for her departure. The house would soon be filling up with their children and grandchildren, and as long as she stayed, her presence was more and more likely to be the cause of rumours.

By mid-morning she heard them moving about upstairs, and knocked on their door. Douglas was still in his dressing gown but welcomed her in with his usual warmth.

'It's Bastille Day on the fourteenth. The village celebrates with a magnificent feast,' he said, when she told them she was thinking of leaving. 'Stay at least for that. You'll have some good memories to take with you.'

The fourteenth was only the following Saturday, and she agreed.

Preparations were already starting for the feast. Tables and chairs were delivered in lorries and stacked up against the church. A huge spit arrived for roasting a sheep, and lights were being strung through the trees that lined the square. The young people who gathered each evening on the steps of the chapel at the far end of the village, became even more animated than usual, and the inexhaustible conversations of the old, who favoured the square's benches or brought chairs to sit outside their houses, seemed more tireless than ever. Talk was also lively between the women gathered around the boules piste by the war memorial to watch the players, as they debated the arrangement of tables and who was going to sit where. Even the cyclists who paused for refreshment in the café after their long climb up from the coast, asked curiously what was going on.

She hadn't seen Clemence for the last few days, until they met for coffee in the café that afternoon. She told her her husband and daughter had just returned from

Marseille, and she was also busy with preparations for the feast. Everyone was expected to contribute to the menu drawn up by a committee of local women and distributed to each household to tick off the dishes they'd be providing. Jessie asked what she could offer and Clemence replied that salads were always welcome and she could sign her up for that, to which Jessie agreed.

When she re-entered the house, delicious smells of cooking reached her and she went upstairs to find Ruth surrounded by quiche bases, jointed carcasses of chicken and hare, bunches of wild herbs, strings of onions and garlic, and vegetables of all kinds, together with a pile of brioches fresh from the oven.

'Wow! How many people are you planning to feed?' Jessie asked.

Ruth wiped the hair from her damp forehead with her wrist, since her hands were floury.

'Don't worry. It'll all get eaten,' she said, with a smile.

'Clemence told me to make a salad. A bit of a cop out, I think.'

'No, salads are good. They take time to prepare and have to be done at the last minute. That's why they're not popular with the cooks.'

'Right. Well, I better leave you to it.'

She turned to go, but paused in the doorway.

'Is it just the villagers for this feast or do people come from further field?'

Ruth shook her head.

'This one's just for us.'

Jessie felt relief. At least that minimised the danger of running into Paolo and his wife.

She went down to the beach for a swim. Tourists from Italy and Germany were starting to arrive, but the real crowds were not due till the end of the month. As she looked for a good place to lay out her towel, she saw Simon approaching. The sun had darkened his skin and he looked relaxed and handsome. She thought, not for the first time, what an attractive man he was and wondered if he had a girlfriend.

'I hear you're leaving us after the feast,' he said, sitting down beside her. 'It's a shame. But I understand.'

'You'll need the flat for the rest of your family,' she replied, ignoring the implication of his last remark.

'Ah, yes! A house full of screaming kids and my warring sisters-in-law.'

'Oh dear. You don't sound as if you're looking forward to it.'

'Don't get me wrong. I love my brothers, and their wives and children are ok in smallish doses. Anyway, there's always somewhere I can retreat to. Don't forget I grew up here.'

'Yes, that must have been wonderful. Have you ever thought of returning?'

'Full-time?'

He shook his head.

She understood so little about the pressures of growing up on the island. Coming from English and Canadian parents, the need to prove himself more Corsican than the Corsicans, to speak their language, and to live according to their rules must have been tough. His love for the place was clearly deep rooted, but there would have been struggles and dangers for a young boy that she found hard to imagine.

'Flaubert, I read somewhere, called the island, "Grave and ardent, all black and red",' she said.

'Pretty accurate! Also I can't work here. And there's not much cultural life.'

'No, I guess not.'

He paused.

'This world's too enclosed for people like me.'

She looked at him enquiringly.

'Gay people, those for whom traditional family life isn't an option. My friends tolerate me while I'm here, and I don't rub it in their faces. But I can never truly be one of them, and they know it.'

The thought that Simon was gay had never occurred to Jessie, though now he'd said so it didn't surprise her. There was an ease and openness about him, unusual amongst heterosexual men, especially Corsicans. She wondered how long he'd known it himself and whether during his childhood he'd felt out of place in such a macho culture. She wanted to ask more, but didn't feel she had the right.

'It's meant a lot to me, living here in your house. And having you and Clemence as friends. I don't think I've ever been so happy.'

Or so sad, she added to herself.

'I wanted you to know that.'

'I'm glad to hear it. It can't have been easy, coming back after what you'd been through before.'

'Maybe, but it was also what I needed to do.' She smiled. 'Lay the ghost, so to speak.'

'And has it? Laid the ghost?'

'Yes, I think so. It's also given me a lot to think about. What I really want to do with my life.'

'So that's good?'

'I believe it is.'

He'd made no mention of Paolo, for which she was grateful. The last thing she wanted him, or anyone else, to know about was her reckless visit to the Niolo. She seemed to be holding her breath as each day went by without news of him, or of any further catastrophe. But nothing could put her mind at rest.

On the way home she stopped off at the local supermarket and stocked up on ingredients for a variety of salads, which would keep for a day in her fridge. The square was now closed to cars, so she drove to the schoolyard below the road, where cars were parked when the village ran out of space.

As she pulled into a space, she saw Clemence getting out of her car, with her husband and daughter. From the number of bags they were carrying it looked as though they'd been shopping in town. They greeted one another with a kiss on both cheeks, then Jessie shook hands with Thierry and Amal. As they turned to go, Clemence said,

'Can I drop by a bit later? Say 6?'

'Of course.'

'See you then,' she said, and followed her family up the short hill to the road.

Inside the flat Jessie unpacked her shopping and stuffed the salads into the fridge. She wondered why

Clemence had asked to see her and whether it was something special. The thought made her slightly nervous.

It was 6.15 when she heard the front door open and close then footsteps on the stone stairs. A moment later there was a knock on her door and she hurried to open it. Clemence stood there, clutching a newspaper in her hand.

They went through to the terrace, where she'd laid out glasses, a bottle of rosé and some olives, and sat down on either side of the table.

'Would you like a drink?'

'Thanks,' Clemence said.

She poured them each a glass, whilst Clemence spread out the copy of Corse Matin on the table, and turned to one of the middle pages. A large photograph of a funeral filled most of the page. A hearse was proceeding along a village street, followed by a long procession of mourners dressed in black. First came men in suits and berets, some carrying rifles, and behind them women, some veiled and carrying posies of flowers, and children, the boys in suits and girls in Sunday dresses. After the chief mourners a host of people, also in mourning, followed. It looked like over a hundred people.

'D'you recognise anyone?' Clemence said.

Jessie looked closer but shook her head.

'Read what it says below.'

Jessie pulled the paper towards her and read,

"Today the funeral took place in the Niolo valley of Ermano Savelli, beloved brother of Paolo Savelli, mayor of

Casamaccioli. Loyal fighter for the FLNC, defender of our liberty, may he rest in peace."

Jessie felt the blood drain from her face, as a huge feeling of relief swept over her. She peered again at the photo, and saw what she felt sure was Paolo, following the coffin. He was safe!

'Does it say what Ermano died of?'

Clemence leaned over her shoulder to point out what was written on the opposite page.

'Here... It says it was a hunting accident... I think that's Paolo.' She pointed at the photo. 'And that's Marie-Paule and their son, right behind the hearse.'

Together they scrutinised the image. Then Jessie sat back in her chair.

'D'you believe that about a hunting accident?'

Clemence shrugged.

'It happens. Who knows?'

'I don't believe it for a minute.'

'So what d'you think happened?'

She shook her head.

'It doesn't really matter. As long as Paolo had nothing to do with it.'

'These are mountain people, Jessie. They've spent their lives fighting and feuding with each other. Who knows what grudges they hold between them? And anyway, it may well have been an accident.'

Jessie was silent. She was thinking of how she might be able to contact Paolo, find out how he was. But that was even less possible when the family would be drawn together, tighter than ever in their time of mourning.

'I have to go. I told Thierry and Amal I'd be back for

supper. I just wanted you to know about this before someone else told you... You can feel safe now.'

Jessie reached for Clemence's hand.

'Thanks.'

At the kitchen door they embraced, then Clemence was gone.

Jessie returned to the terrace. Ermano's death meant she no longer had to fear him. But in another sense it resolved nothing. She thought of the last time she'd seen the two brothers together, Paolo doing his best to hold down Ermano and ordering her to leave while she could. She'd known the fight between them had escalated to an even more dangerous level. What if after she'd left, Paolo had killed him? Fratricide was a crime no one could get over. It ruined the lives of the survivors and in a small community like theirs would never be forgotten. The thought made her feel sick.

After a largely sleepless night, she got up early, made herself coffee and took it out onto the terrace. Before going to bed she'd stuffed the paper into a drawer, not wanting to be confronted with it in the morning. There was another day to get through before the Bastille feast and most people would be busy with their preparations. She decided to drive up the coast to a small bay, from where a path led round to a promontory and an island you could swim across to, inhabited only by birds.

She packed some sandwiches, a bottle of water, and a towel into her backpack, put on her swimsuit under her shorts and teeshirt, picked up her sunhat and made her way to the school yard to collect the car.

A small road that ended in an unpaved track descended from the main coastal road, winding its way past a cluster of discreet villas hidden between shade trees, and across a single-track railway line to the sea. On the far side of the railway was space for parking a few cars. From there she picked up the coastal path that ran along the edge of the bay. It was early and so far no other human being was to be seen. The day would soon grow hot, but for now the sun on her skin felt pleasantly warm and a breeze blew in from the sea.

She resisted the temptation to go for a bathe in the lagoon-like waters of the first bay, and pressed on knowing she'd a long walk ahead of her if she wanted to reach the island before the sun grew too hot. The path followed the rough shape of the coast line, winding past rocks and between tufts of myrtle, here and there descending into a small gulley, before flattening out once more into open moorland filled with wild flowers and the scent of herbs.

Perched above the promontory was the ruin of one of the Martello towers that peppered the coastline, lookouts built by the Genoans, who for centuries had dominated the island. She skirted the steepest part and climbed round onto flat rocks, worn smooth by sea and wind, that formed the near side of the channel. The distance between the promontory and the island was only a couple of hundred metres and easily swimmable.

She took off her shorts and teeshirt and stuffed them into her backpack, took a long swig of water from the bottle she'd brought and walked to the edge of the rock. The water below was deep and so clear she could see small fishes darting hither and thither over the stones. She dived in, shocked momentarily by the cold, and swam towards the island.

Halfway across the channel, she turned onto her back to rest. Out of the corner of her eye, she glimpsed the glossy flank of a large fish not more than ten metres away. She rolled back onto her front and trod water to get a better view. The fish seemed to be circling her, diving then surfacing again in a way that could only be described as playful. Suddenly it leapt fully out of the water, and for a moment she saw the sleek body of a magnificent blue-black porpoise. She laughed out loud with delight and raised an arm in salutation, as it plunged back into the sea with a loud splash.

When she reached the island, she waded ashore, a narrow strip of shingle ending in tufts of pink-flowered sea scabious that rose steeply upwards to a rocky knoll, stained all over with guano from the myriad sea birds nesting there. She looked back across the channel then further out to sea, hoping to catch another sight of the porpoise, but he had vanished. She was filled with a deep sense of pride and joy, as though that magnificent inhabitant of the deep had for a moment come to greet her. She sat on the shore, alert to every sound and change of light, breathing in the scents of wild rosemary that edged the gritty sand, until eventually she felt the sun burning her shoulders and re-entered the water.

Driving back to the village she was aware of something new, a feeling of detachment in which she hardly recognised herself. It was as though she were suspended between one state of being and another, and for the first time in a long while her thoughts turned tentatively towards home.

On re-entering the house, she heard Ruth calling out to come upstairs.

'Since you've decided to leave us, Douglas and I would like to do something special for you.'

'That's lovely of you. But won't the Bastille dinner be special enough? Anything more and I'll be too sad to leave!'

'Well, you promise to be back?'

'Absolutely!'

'Then let's make sure we earmark places at our table for those you'd most like to sit with.'

'Ok... You and Douglas, Simon, Clemence, Thierry and Amal (unless she'd rather be with her friends). And perhaps Etienne, if he's invited.'

'Of course.'

Ruth jotted down the names on a piece of paper.

'By the way, what should I wear?'

'Something festive. The more extravagant, the better!'

'So what will you be wearing?'

'Ah, that's a surprise!'

Jessie returned to her flat, wondering what on earth she could find that was suitable for the feast. She'd only brought the most basic wardrobe – shorts and teeshirts, a pair of jeans, a silk shirt, and a couple of summer dresses, nothing fit for a special party. She decided to ask

Clemence if she could lend her something or at least suggest how she might spice up the few garments she had.

In the afternoon she went to look for Clemence in the café, and failing to find her, left a message on her mobile for her to call. Half an hour later she did so. She sounded harassed, and Jessie could hear voices in the background and the clashing of pots and pans.

'Sorry to disturb you. You're obviously busy,' Jessie said.

'Thierry and Amal are cooking for tomorrow. I've done my stuff. Do you need something?'

'Your advice. I've nothing to wear for the feast.'

'I'll come over. I'll be only too glad to get out of this mayhem.'

Twenty minutes later Jessie heard the front door open and footsteps on the stairs. She opened the kitchen door to receive Clemence, laden with two large plastic bags stuffed full of clothes. She led the way to the dining room and Clemence dumped the bags onto the daybed. She opened them up to reveal garments of all shapes and colours – tunics, shirts, tops, harem trousers, dresses, a little silk jacket, an embroidered cap, and several long, coloured scarves.

'Right,' she said. 'Let's see what you fancy.'

'My God! It looks like some Eastern bazaar!'

'Plenty to choose from.'

Jessie fetched the long mirror from her bedroom and together they began sorting through the clothes, selecting one garment after another and holding them up against her to see the effect. Eventually they settled on a pair of crimson harem trousers, a sleeveless cream top, the short, silk jacket with a long, chiffon scarf wound around her throat, and the embroidered cap.

'There! You look like an Eastern princess,' Clemence said, as Jessie studied herself in the mirror.

'I think I look more like a boy.'

'Prince, then. Nothing sexier than androgyny! Hang on a minute!'

She rootled in her handbag and brought out a black eye liner. She turned Jessie to face her and began drawing lines to exaggerate her eyes, followed by a fine, pencil moustache with upturned ends.

Turning back to the mirror, Jessie contemplated her reflection. She struck a couple of strutting male poses, and burst into laughter.

'Ok! Your turn,' she cried.

Clemence took off her jeans and teeshirt, chose a tight, low-cut dress that showed off her figure and tied a scarf turban-style around her unruly hair.

'Now the makeup!' Jessie said and, grabbing her makeup bag from the bathroom, applied eye liner, rouge and lipstick in excess, until Clemence resembled some exotic beauty from a theatrical harem. Together they swanned around the room in a solemn dance, making ever more lewd and exotic gestures, until at length they collapsed onto the daybed, joyful and exhausted.

Eventually, Jessie sat up.

'This calls for a real drink.'

She disappeared into the kitchen and returned with a bottle of malt whisky, a bowl of ice, and two glasses on a tray. Clemence followed her out onto the terrace, Jessie poured whisky, added ice, and took one glass for herself, holding the other out to Clemence.

'To good times to come! And to friendship!'

'Amen to that!' Clemence said, and they clinked glasses.

Bastille Day began with a procession. Eight sturdy men carried the Virgin Mary from the church on a platform through the narrow streets from one end of the village to the other, followed by a choir of village children singing praises to the Holy Mother. Behind them parents and grandparents brought up the rear. After them came an assortment of villagers, the older women in their customary sombre black, the men in dark suits and sometimes a beret. Donning festive finery was to come with the lunch.

After the procession people returned to their homes to prepare for the main event, except for an ever-growing number of helpers, busy setting out chairs and laying tables.

The spit with a whole sheep had already been roasting for an hour or so, and delicious scents of roasted meat filled the square. As Jessie stepped out of the front door of the house, she could feel the buzz of excitement and anticipation. It reminded her of the day of the fête, when she had first seen Paolo. Today he was in mourning, so there was no chance he would be at the feast. It meant she was safe to enjoy herself with her friends, though the memory of his presence on that other occasion brought a sharp pang of regret. She determined not to think of him and to concentrate on the scene before her.

More and more people were emerging from their houses, dressed in their finery and bearing plates of charcuterie and cheeses, pots of cooked meat or vegetables, huge salads of local olives with tomatoes and basil, flasks of newly pressed olive oil and breads of all shapes and sizes, still hot from the oven. She saw Clemence carrying plates to the table that had been commandeered for them, not far from Douglas and Ruth's front door. She was dressed in a sleeveless dress of emerald green, that suited her rich colouring, with a short bolero embroidered with lace and sequins, and into her dark hair she had pinned a purple orchid. Jessie thought how beautiful and elegant she looked. Her own costume by contrast seemed overdone and outlandish, but it was too late now. She ran back inside to fetch the salads she'd made, and on returning placed them beside the other dishes along the centre of the table.

The square was filling up and people beginning to take their seats. Thierry was already seated when Douglas and Ruth emerged from the house to join them. Amal had elected to sit with a group of young people on the other side of the church. A few minutes later Simon appeared, accompanied by Etienne, beside whom Jessie found herself placed. It was always a pleasure, she thought, to talk to Etienne.

Once most people were settled, Philippe Savelli stood up from his table next to the church steps, and with a microphone in his hand began to address the crowd.

'Welcome all, friends, family, and honoured guests, to

this great feast! The celebration of July 14th 1789 is to honour the liberty of France, liberty that must be forever cherished so that each part of our great republic may continue to live together in peace and harmony!'

He went on to speak more specifically of Corsica and Pascale Paoli, that great proponent of liberty and good governance in the vein of Tom Paine, men who understood the importance of co-operation without dependence. The audience began to grow restive, as they eyed the rapidly cooling dishes before them, and Marie-Josef nudged her husband discreetly. With a brief glance in her direction, he brought his speech to a slightly hurried close, and after a short round of applause the eating and drinking began.

The food was delicious, the roasted sheep was handed round by young servers, and the wine flowed. At length everyone at Jessie's table had cleared their plates and sat back to enjoy a short respite, before it was time to gather them up and clear the table for the next course.

Ruth, Simon and Thierry returned to their respective houses, to exchange empty dishes for platters of dessert, jugs of cream and baskets of fruit, whilst across the table Clemence and Douglas remained deep in conversation. Etienne reached into the pocket of his satchel that hung over the back of his chair, and took out a long, slender package wrapped in cloth. He turned to Jessie.

'This is the moment, I think, to give you these.'

He handed her the parcel, then from an inner pocket of his jacket produced an envelope and pressed it into her other hand.

'Hide them away for now.'

She laid the parcel across her knees, hidden by the table, and stuffed the envelope into the pocket of her trousers, hoping Douglas and Clemence hadn't noticed the blush that suffused her cheeks. She knew at once who the gifts were from.

'How did you get them?' she asked Etienne quietly.

'A soldier in my unit brought them. Said he knew I was coming to the feast today and had been asked if I could deliver them to you.'

Jessie was too shaken to reply. Etienne took hold of her hand and gripped it tight for a brief moment. She looked up at him, her eyes moist.

'We can talk later, if you want. Tomorrow maybe,' he said.

Ruth appeared from the house, carrying a tray laden with sweetmeats. Etienne stood up, took the tray from her, and carried it to the table. Simon and Thierry returned, bearing more desserts and special wines to go with them, and attention was once more focussed on the delights before them.

Eventually, when the children had finished eating and were chasing joyfully in and out of the tables, some people began exchanging places to talk with friends and neighbours, whilst others cleared away dishes, replenished drinks or brought coffee from their houses. Jessie could contain her impatience no longer. Clemence, Thierry and Simon had already moved elsewhere, and Etienne was engaged in conversation with Douglas and Ruth. She excused herself briefly and, clutching her parcel to her, returned to the house. Inside, she ran upstairs and threw open the kitchen door of her apartment, closing it firmly behind her. She laid the parcel on the table in the dining room and carefully began to remove the cloth covering, layer by layer until the finely polished surface of a flute was revealed.

At once she recognised Paolo's pipe. She ran her fingers gently over it, following its contours. It was a beautifully made instrument, with finely sculpted mouthpiece and each stop lined with a thin strip of dark wood, like ebony. She picked it up and cradled it between her hands, its weight lightly resting between her upturned palms. She recalled the last time she'd heard its clear, resonant voice that followed her across fields and woods all the way to the road. She could picture him now on the hill above his farm, seated on a large stone surrounded by his goats, a timeless figure not unlike Pan himself. And now he had sent the pipe to her.

She laid it down on its cloths and pulled the letter out of her pocket, tore open the envelope and spread out the paper inside.

"My dearest Jessie, when you read this letter, you will also have received the pipe I sent with it. Over twenty years ago I made a simple pipe for you, using my then very limited skills. It told you it was my attempt to give you back your voice, the voice we had taken from you. And you learned to make it speak.

When you left me the other day, you asked me to play for you as you went. You said it would be as though I were still speaking to you.

This pipe is my truest voice. Play it, as I know you can, and through it we may continue to talk to each other, my voice merging with yours. Music, as we both know, is a language more universal than any other, where we can continue to be present for one another. And perhaps we will find comfort there, even in absence. You will always be in my heart, Paolo."

She sat on the daybed, clutching the pipe to her and sobbed as though her heart would break.

Later, when the sun had gone down, she made herself a cup of tea with herbs from the maquis, and took it out onto the terrace. The sun had gone down and the mountain was losing its colour as the light faded. It felt slightly chilly after the heat of the day, so she fetched a sweater. The storm of weeping was over, leaving her swept clean, empty of emotion. She sat gazing out over the darkening valley, conscious only of the blood flowing through her veins and a light throbbing in her temples, as deep, slow breaths came and went. She gazed up at the vast, star-speckled heavens, and listened with her inner ear to the faint pulsating harmony of the music of the spheres.

———

Going home

In the morning she booked a ferry for the evening in two days' time and a train ticket to London, and went upstairs to tell Ruth and Douglas.

'In that case we must celebrate!' Douglas exclaimed.

'Obviously not your departure!' Ruth said.

'Of course not. Your time here, our friendship, and your speedy return!' Douglas retorted. 'And I know just the place.'

Jessie looked at him expectantly but he shook his head.

'It'll be a surprise. Tomorrow evening. And wear your best clothes! Not fancy dress!'

'Something a bit more sober. But we loved your costume yesterday!'

The next person Jessie needed to talk to was Clemence, and by late morning she went in search of her. She wasn't in the café or anywhere in the village, so she went to her house and knocked on the door. She'd rarely been to Clemence's tall, cramped house, squashed between others on what was more of a steep alley than a street. As there was no room for gardens, the inhabitants had filled the spaces outside their front doors with tubs of flowers and herbs. Some also brought chairs to sit out there, making the narrow passage impassable to cars.

It was a while before the door was opened by Thierry.

'I hope this isn't a bad time,' Jessie said, smiling. 'I'm leaving tomorrow and wanted to wish you all goodbye.'

'Come in. I'll fetch Clemence,' he said, holding the door open for her to pass through.

The house inside was chaotic, as though someone had randomly chucked their belongings onto every piece of furniture, including the floor.

'Forgive the mess,' Thierry said briskly. 'Clemence and Amal have been having a bit of a clear out.'

'I can see!' Jessie said, picking her way through the debris on her way to the kitchen, where he invited her to sit down.

'Can I get you a coffee?'

'A glass of water, please. I'm coffee-ed out!'

'Ok. I'll call her.'

He brought her the water then disappeared, pulling the door to after him.

Jessie looked around the room. Compared to the hallway and living room, it was relatively tidy, but she felt a tension in the house that made her uncomfortable. As soon as Clemence appeared she'd try to persuade her to come out.

A couple of minutes later Clemence came into the room. Her eyes looked puffy and her face was more heavily made up than usual, as if to hide the effects of weeping.

'If this is a bad time I can leave. I just wanted to see you, maybe take you out for a drink. I'm leaving the day after tomorrow.'

Clemence went to her and threw her arms about her. They hugged each other close, and Jessie heard a catch in her breath, as if she were stifling a sob. But when she pulled away, she was dry-eyed.

'Yes. I'd like that. I'll just tell Thierry. I'll meet you at the café.'

As Jessie walked down the steep, winding street to the square and on to the café, she thought about what she'd just seen. Clemence obviously wasn't happy, but she didn't want to make things worse by being overly sympathetic or encouraging anger or resentment.

She sat down at a table under a tree on the small café terrace and ordered a couple of local beers, and after a few minutes Clemence arrived.

'You're leaving so soon!' she said, sitting down.

'I'm afraid so. But perhaps you can come and see me in London. Later in the summer?'

'I'd like that. Maybe when the school term starts and we're back in Marseille.'

Jessie nodded, and for a moment neither of them spoke.

'What's going on?' Jessie said at length, abandoning her resolution not to interfere. She couldn't keep silent when Clemence was so obviously suffering.

'Nothing new. It's the anniversary of Julien's death. We both find that hard, but somehow we aren't able to comfort one another.'

Jessie reached for her hand and she gripped it back.

'People say time makes it easier. I find it makes little difference.'

Jessie thought of Paolo. But losing him was not the same as losing a child.

'I know I should concentrate on Amal, how unfair it is on her who never even knew Julien. And naturally she resents my being so distracted. I thank God Thierry's able to love her as she should be loved.'

Jessie held her gaze.

'You know, it took me a long time to love Stephanie... But still it is a real love I feel, a closeness and affection nothing can destroy, not even the ending of marriage to her father.'

Clemence held her hand fast.

'There's something else I want to tell you.' Jessie paused. 'Paolo's sent me a gift. His pipe. I can't tell you how much that means to me.'

Clemence looked up.

'He made it, and it's a work of great beauty and real skill.'

'And will you play it?'

'Of course! Sometimes I play with a group of other musicians in London, and I can take it with me instead of my clarinet.'

'I think that's wonderful. You must tell him!'

'I don't think that'll be possible.'

'Why not? Make him a recording. You can send it to his iphone without any message. He'll know it's from you, and if anyone was suspicious, he could claim he'd just come across it on YouTube.'

'What a wonderful idea!'

'You see! I'm full of them!' Clemence said, smiling.

Jessie leaned across and hugged her.

'When you come to London, you can come and hear us play. There's lots of other fun things, of course. You must make a list of what you'd like to do most. And you can meet Stephanie. She's the same age as Amal.'

The prospect of a visit to London appeared visibly to cheer Clemence, and Jessie ordered another couple of beers.

'If you're free this afternoon we could go down to the beach. I need to get my fill of that glorious sea before I leave.'

'Ok. Thierry and Amal have plans to go into L'Île-

Rousse for some clothes shopping. I guess they can do without me.'

Ruth had left a note, asking her to meet them at the front door at eight that evening. They could all go to the surprise venue in one car.

Returning from the beach, she spent the rest of the afternoon packing and cleaning up the flat, then showered, washed her hair, and changed into her nicest dress, strappy sandals with low heels, and the beautiful chiffon scarf Clemence had given her following the Bastille feast.

As they drove along the coast road, the sun had already begun its descent. After three or four kilometres, they turned onto a small side road that wound its way down towards the shore, ending in a carpark shaded by tamarind trees. Steps led to a small, sheltered bay that faced across the wide expense of water to the distant lights of Calvi. The bay was bordered by huge, flat rocks with tufts of wild scabious and sea kale, over which the coastal path continued onwards to a small promontory, topped by a Martello tower. Tables were spread out on the sand, and behind them a low building housed more tables and the restaurant's kitchen. Blackboards on stands were set out at intervals on the sand, on which an elaborate menu had been chalked.

A waiter in an immaculate white apron welcomed them and led them to their table. Several were already occupied by couples and the odd family, some embracing three generations. The clientele were casually elegant and prosperous-looking, far more so than Jessie was used to on the island, and they were obviously at home here.

Etienne was already seated at their table with a glass of wine and a book. He stood up to greet them and pulled out a seat for Ruth.

'You made it in time for the sunset!' he said.

Jessie searched in her bag for her sunglasses and sat down. The sun had become a great golden ball, turning the western sea to molten gold, and the sky red, apricot and purple, fading to green and duck egg blue at the edges. It was a sunset more spectacular than any she had seen, and everyone had turned to face it, transfixed by its magnificence. Jessie kicked off her sandals and curled her toes into the gritty sand beneath her feet, as she watched the great ball of light make its slow descent into an ever-darkening sea.

When at length the last rind of colour had disappeared below the horizon, an audible sigh went up from the crowd and attention turned to food. The hovering waiters hurried forward bearing chalked boards, eager to explain their cornucopia of delights.

'What exactly is this place?' Jessie asked, after they had given their orders. 'Why has no one mentioned it before?'

Douglas laughed.

'Those they want to know, do so. They're never short of customers!'

He gestured towards the other diners.

'The location is fabulous and it's the only place to eat really good food. No doubt you've discovered what a rarity that is here,' Ruth said.

'Even the waiters are charming!' Jessie said, laughing.

'"Everything should contribute to the pleasure of the dining experience!", according to the old patron,' Douglas declared. 'He was a high-up member of Corsica Libera, a real character and, by the way, a great chess player. Etienne and I would often join him here for a game, and were rewarded with a fine dinner – free if he won. Now its run by the new breed of inheritors and the prices are even higher. But the food's just as good and the location as beautiful, so we still enjoy coming from time to time.'

'It's utterly magical!'

'A good way to spend your last evening on the island,' Ruth said.

Jessie smiled her agreement.

Two more delicious courses followed, interposed by tiny plates of savoury fish, thimbles of exquisitely distilled consommé of meat or vegetables, even a spoonful of delicately flavoured water ice topped by a sprig of mint to cleanse the palate. The chef, Jessie thought, must be some kind of alchemist to create dishes of such perfection.

Whilst they ate, the three of them regaled Jessie with stories of their adventures on coming to the island, the characters they'd encountered and scrapes they'd got into.

'Corsica then was almost untouched by life on the continent,' Douglas said. 'There were few cars and not many tourists, because it was hard to get around with no decent roads. What fragments of coastal road that existed, all ended abruptly after a few kilometres, and the only way to go south was to drive north to the interior and travel down the island's central spine. Which of course is still the case.'

'And on the way you passed through primeval forests

of magnificent ancient trees, a few of which have survived the endless rounds of fires,' Ruth added.

Jessie thought of her own experience of coming here more than twenty years ago. To her, too, the island had seemed like another world, one that was primitive and untouched.

'Despite its remoteness, this restaurant could easily compete with the best France can offer,' she said.

'True,' Etienne replied, adding, 'For the mafia, only the very best!'

By the time they rose to go, a crescent moon had risen, reflected in the inky dark of the sea. Jessie took the arm Etienne offered to guide her up the steps from the beach to the car, where they said their final goodbyes. He was someone whose friendship she would have liked to maintain, though that seemed unlikely unless something one day brought her back to the island.

As she sat alone in the back of Douglas and Ruth's car, she thought about the friendships she'd made since coming here, brief encounters that could not be held onto but no less memorable for that. The exception, she hoped, was Clemence. She'd promised to visit her in London, and she would hold her to her promise.

The evening at the restaurant had been a perfect ending to her visit. But it was also evidence of how much the island was changing. The distinctive way of life Ermano and his comrades fought so hard to defend was under increasing threat from ever-expanding tourism, destruction of fertile land and olive groves by fires, both climate-generated and those caused by man that plagued the island, and the accompanying rise in land values.

Caught in the middle was Paolo, struggling to find a path between the destruction of so much he and his fellows cherished, and the need to open up to the modern world. Some areas stood out against the greed of the developers, and no doubt the Niolo was one. But for how long, she wondered?

When she got home, she thanked Douglas and Ruth for a wonderful evening and climbed the stairs to her apartment. Inside she sought out her diary and turned to the last page, a brief coda she'd written after her return home. It described her homecoming and the joy of being reunited with her mother, who'd prepared a special cele-bratory supper.

I thanked Mum for the splendid feast she'd made. Then suddenly she asked, 'What was she like, this Mama?' It was a question I dreaded, though I wasn't sure why. I wanted to tell her how despite everything I'd come to love this woman, but I didn't want to seem disloyal. I told her she was strict but nice. A big woman and strong, even though she was no longer young. She could get angry but she also had a good sense of humour and never actually mistreated me. In fact, she was my protector. And you should have heard her sing! I guess you could say I grew quite fond of her, I said. And though she didn't reply, Mum seemed to understand.

Then she asked me about the others and I told her I hated her sons. Except for Paolo. He was different. I'd never met anyone like him before, and I can't bear to think of him in prison. But equally I can't imagine him away from Corsica.

He'd be lost over here, degraded somehow. Even more lost than I was over there.

She laid the diary down and gazed out over the dark land. Tomorrow she would take the ferry from L'Île-Rousse and in the morning the train from Nice to London. The sounds of scope owls and faint scurryings of insects and small creatures in the undergrowth, together with the scents of the maquis from the cooling earth after the heat of the day, filled her with a pleasant languor. She felt neither grief nor elation, as though part of her had already started on the journey home. And yet something would always remain, if in imagination only. Whatever trauma her time of captivity had caused had been laid to rest, and though the love she felt for Paolo was undiminished, it would gradually lose its power to hurt.

She went back into the dining room to look for the CD she'd bought of A Filetta, and found it on the dining table, together with her old Walkman. She picked them up, took a bottle of rosé from the fridge, and returned to the terrace. She poured herself a glass of wine, inserted the disc into the Walkman and sat back in her chair. The high nasal voice of the lead singer soared above his fellows in harmonies that echoed back to lost Saracen invaders, recalled and reinvented by generations of shepherds that still roamed these hills and valleys with their flocks. Their music filled the night with haunting cries of human longing, suffering, and joy, calling down the centuries with a power that never ceased to stir the soul.

READ THE PREQUEL

OUT OF STEP

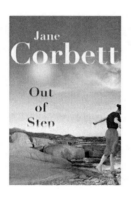

Over twenty years earlier, the struggle for Corsican independence was at its height, something which most tourists to the island were happily unaware. 16 year old Fleur, (who later prefers to be known by her middle name, Jessie) is very excited to be invited to the island on holiday with the family of a school friend. There on the beach she meets a handsome local boy, and hoping for the holiday romance of her dreams, she accepts his invitation to go for a walk. But it is a trap, and she is seized and held captive for three weeks by local partisans. *Out of Step* tells the story of an ordeal that will shape Fleur's life for years to come.

187

A SHORT HISTORY OF CORSICA

The island of Corsica, a gem set in a glittering blue sea, has a turbulent history. Its position has always made it an object of desire to surrounding nations, for whoever controlled Corsica could dominate the Western Mediterranean. For the island and its people, this meant centuries of war and strife, invasion and occupation.

In earliest times the invaders were Greeks, Carthaginians and Romans; in the Dark Ages, Vandals and Ostrogoths; at the time of the Crusades, the Saracen raiders. Even in comparatively peaceful times, the feudal lords quarrelled among themselves and their rule over the people was harsh and oppressive.

In desperation the people appealed to the Pope, who sent Lodolphe, the Archbishop of Pisa in Italy, to govern the island. Under the Pisan administration during the 12 th and 13 th centuries there was relative calm. But the power of Pisa was soon challenged by another Italian city state, Genoa, resulting in constant battles in which the Corsican feudal lords frequently changed allegiance.

The Genoese eventually gained the upper hand and ruled Corsica from 1347 until the late 1700s. They proved harsh overlords, who exploited the land even worse than the feudal lords. The Corsican hero Sampiero led an uprising against them, but they killed him and redoubled their harsh rule. The people suffered bitterly from excessive taxation, famine and poverty. Hunger and desperation forced many to emigrate to the Continent.

In 1729 a guerrilla war of independence began, and the Corsicans asked for help from the French. With the cooperation of one of the most enlightened men ever to rule the island, Pascal Paoli, they finally gained control of it, and Paoli remains a popular hero to this day. Eventually, however, he fell out with the French rulers and created a brief allegiance with the British and Lord Nelson, (who lost his eye at the siege of Calvi during the French Revolutionary Wars). But in 1796 Paoli and the British were ousted, and the island fell to the French. Napoleon, a Corsican from Ajaccio, became the conqueror of Europe, and to this day French remains the official language of Corsica.

Over the years the feeling has grown that the French have ignored the loyalty of the Corsican people through two World Wars, and neglected their responsibility towards them. In the Second World War, the island was occupied by 80,000 Italians, with the help of 10,000 Germans, and as a result the town of Bastia was bombed by both the Germans and the Allies. But the Corsicans remained loyal to the French. They had a strong partisan movement, who maintained contact with the Free French, and the guerrilla tactics learned during this period continued to serve the Independence Movement after the war ended.

In 1962 at the end of the Algerian War, the French government allotted considerable portions of Corsican land to ex-colonialists (pieds noirs) who wished to leave Algeria. This added to the Corsican people's sense of injustice, of being treated as a colony to be exploited according to the whim of their masters. Corsicans continued to be forced into economic exile, as the fight for a still unrealised independence intensified.

ALSO BY JANE CORBETT

The Last Musketeer

Looking for Home

Beasts and Lovers

ABOUT THE AUTHOR

Jane Corbett studied English at Newham College, Cambridge, and is the author of a YA novel *Out of Step*, a volume of modern fairy tales titled *Beasts and Lovers*, and several award-winning screenplays. In the seventies she taught at the progressive Kingsway College, including among her students John Lydon and Timothy Spall. Now, she runs workshops for writers and filmmakers and teaches documentary filmmaking at the National Film and Television School. Her other passions are horse riding, yoga and her grandson. She lives in London with her husband.

www.janecorbett-writer.com